SACRIFICIAL
LAMBS

BY SHERI WHITE

"I still don't understand, Abby. How are you planning to help us?" Sheila was tingling with anticipation; she had the feeling this woman could help her in some way. She felt almost hopeful, an unfamiliar emotion of late.

Abby sank down in a chair facing the group. "After Jenna was taken and everything finally settled down, it occurred to me that my problem had been solved in an extremely tidy manner. Unlike Downs and Smith, someone else really had taken my daughter. I wasn't under any suspicion, I had the sympathy of the community, and I got my life back—it was perfect."

Jackie, the black woman, jumped up from her seat. "Wait a minute—are you telling me we should kill our kids? Are you fuckin' kidding me? You are one sick bitch, lady!"

"No, of course not." Abby motioned the woman to sit back down. Jackie reluctantly complied, a look of suspicion on her face. "Haven't you been listening? Women who kill their kids are usually caught. They're sent to prison for life and reviled by the public. You can't get a fresh start that way. But you can start a new life if someone else takes care of the problem for you." She gazed intently at the new members. "We provide that someone else."

Acknowledgments

Thanks to everyone for reading my stories and encouraging me to write more, but especially to my husband Chris and my girls Sarah, Lauren, and Becca who put up with my quirks and anxieties. And a huge thanks and lots of love to my mother-in law/ best friend Anita. You have always believed in me.

Also, thanks to my brother Dave Myles for letting me use his creepy and fantastic photograph for the cover. Check him out at https://www.davemylesphotography.com/.

FOREWORD AND DEDICATION

I started writing quite a bit back in 1999, and even got published several times, much to my delight. That was back in the days of snail-mail submissions and long waiting times.

I got to meet a lot of friends through message boards, attending some conventions, and had a great time as a member of the horror community. But then 9/11 happened, and it shook me to my core. We all know that life is short, but I think 9/11 drilled that into many of us. My kids were still very young at that time (my girls were 3, 6, and 12), and I decided that instead of concentrating so much on writing that I would devote my time to my kids and my husband. It was the right thing to do at the time, but unfortunately, I lost touch with a lot of friends.

Once social networking came into play, I started keeping tabs on the horror community and getting back in touch with friends. Then I saw that Necon E-books was starting a monthly flash fiction contest, and decided it was time to stick my toe back into the water. My girls were older, diaper days were over, and it was time to do something for myself again.

The story I submitted was "The Bridge," and it was a winner of the first Necon E-books contest. I was thrilled. I was sitting in the parking lot of my daughter's high school, waiting for her to put her marching band equipment away, when I checked email on my phone. Matt Bechtel's email congratulating me almost made me cry. Practically ten years of not writing and the first little story I wrote turns out to be a winner.

So I credit Necon E-books with helping me get my shit back together and do what I was meant do.

I'm back in the horror community and back among some

great friends—and my best friend in the biz wrote the foreword for this collection. Monica O'Rourke is not only a great friend, but a kick-ass writer, and a take-no-shit editor. Tony Tremblay is one of my biggest supporters and has encouraged me through all of my writing insecurities. And thank you, Trish Cacek, for helping me to get the ball rolling.

"WHERE IN THE HELL HAVE YOU BEEN?"

BY MONICA O'ROURKE

Imagine my surprise when Sheri White reappeared after falling off the planet for ten years. No one knew what had happened to her, though she was often a favorite topic. There's nothing more fascinating than a missing-persons case.

Around 2002 I owned a small publishing company and became acquainted with her work when an editor kept sending me Sheri White stories. And I kept rejecting them. Not that she was a bad writer but she was raw, and her stories often had undeveloped characters or unsatisfying endings. I think I ended up publishing her because the editor insisted we accept a Sheri White story.

This was around the time she then fell off the planet.

When Sheri reemerged a few years ago it was great to have her back. Our friendship picked up like she'd never left. She'd taken those ten years off to raise her family—but her writing had been on hiatus.

So when she asked me to read a story she wanted to submit to a magazine, I was nervous. Actually, I'm being polite. Although I wanted to encourage her writing, I dreaded reading whatever she was going to send. Didn't she know time hadn't stood still and waited for her to resume? But out of courtesy (and perhaps curiosity) I said I'd read it.

What she sent was somewhat raw—but pretty damned good. So I made a few suggestions (probably more than a few), line edited it, and sent it back, not expecting much of anything. (I don't make that mistake anymore, not with her work.) She tweaked the story, incorporating some suggestions, and sent back something exciting.

That's the best way to describe Sheri's writing these days: exciting.

It seems she's taking the publishing world by storm. Every time I turn around she's winning one writing contest or another or being accepted into some anthology or magazine that would make more seasoned writers jealous.

Many of her plots seem to focus on family, and on loss. You feel the despair in so many of her characters who have to sacrifice in order to save someone they love. It's a maternal, preternatural disposition she seems to share with her characters, a person whose sweetness and kindness come across in the characters and stories she writes. You would think someone like her—someone who is truly *kind*, truly *altruistic* would be writing Hallmark cards or some TV movie starring Kirk Cameron, not stories about people melting, or tossing babies off bridges, or twists on anorexia, or spiders, spiders, and more *spiders!*—not stories that make you cringe, shriek, or grow nauseated as you read. Who is this allegedly quiet, subtle woman, and what is *wrong* with her???

I've come to two conclusions: for those missing ten years, Sheri didn't take time off from writing. She discovered some Himalayan retreat and sneaked off, kidnapped muse in tow, and spent years on the top of the mountains honing her skills.

Actually, that's silly. The more likely reason is that Sheri is a witch, a *bruja*, a preternatural being who isn't quite what she seems. She has us all fooled. Here we see a quiet, unassuming woman with curly light-brown hair, almost a soccer-mom stereotype, raising wonderful daughters somewhere in the sticks. What we actually get is something insane, a mood simmering under a near-boiling pot—and god only knows what she's about to thrown into that pot. I am eternally grateful she uses her talents for good and not evil because one can almost see something devious moving behind her eyes …

So bring it on, Sheri! Show us what you've got! We're not afraid of—

THE FLASH

"The Bridge" is the first story I wrote after years of a writing hiatus. It was a winner in Necon E-books first flash fiction contest. It was a very exciting moment for me. The story was inspired by Maryland's Chesapeake Bay Bridge, a bridge that always make my legs go numb when I have to drive it. There's a perfect view of this beautiful bridge from Sandy Point Beach.

THE BRIDGE

Sandy Point Beach was the perfect spot to watch the mothers throw their newborn baby boys from the Chesapeake Bay Bridge. Sometimes a woman would bring her husband to do this unthinkable act, but it was usually the mother who threw the baby from the bridge. Closure, perhaps.

Jack went to Sandy Point every day, trying to become immune to the wailing and cries of grief from the distraught women. His wife was about to give birth any day. He desperately prayed for a little girl as the screams of mothers and babies surrounded him.

I entered the Necon E-books flash fiction contest again the following month after my first winning entry. Once again, my story was chosen, this time as an honorable mention. The theme was humorous horror. It was a fun one to write.

TRAIN STATION

Oh, look at that chick. All alone in the train station at night. She sure looks upset. Now she's standing right on the edge of the platform. Come on, man—not another one. I already helped a girl a few weeks ago. Who am I, Superman? Fine, I'll help her.

She looked at me as I approached, her eyes wary, yet hopeful. Yes, she wants help. And I'm just in time; the train is just about here.

So I pushed her.

October 2010's flash fiction contest theme was Halloween, of course. I received an honorable mention once again, which mean I had won three times in a row. It really boosted my confidence in my writing.

RECLAIMING HALLOWEEN

I hate this time of year. Fall. September is OK, and so is November, but God, October is awful. Because October is when all the Halloween decorations are put out by everyone in my neighborhood. Artistic Jack-O-Lanterns, rubber bats, fabric witches hitting trees, cutesy smiling scarecrows. Nobody takes Halloween seriously anymore. Children shriek with delight and abandon on Halloween night when they should be shrieking with terror and pain.

This year will be different. I'll put up lame decorations for a change, and buy cheap chocolate bars. They'll come to my house, eager and happy.

I'll be ready.

For the fourth time in a row, my story was chosen as a winner with an honorable mention in the November 2010 contest. The theme was ghost stories. A lot of my stories are from a parent's point of view, and this one was one of them.

MORNING

My little girl wakes me up every morning, jumping on me and giggling. The weight of her crushes me, making it hard to breathe. But her joyful laughter fills my heart with hope and happiness, so I don't tell her to get down. There are days, however, when waking up to this makes me angry; I don't sleep well enough as it is. I never let her know, though. I'd rather kill myself than hurt her feelings. And I'm afraid she'd stop waking me up in the morning.

Then I *would* kill myself.

Because my daughter died last year.

The contest in December 2010 was a difficult one—the theme was Urban Fantasy, and that is not my forte. But I came back in January 2011 since the theme was Open Submissions, and the word count was increased to 250 instead of 100 for the month. This story is another Honorable Mention, and was also published in the anthology 2012 Daily Frights (366 Days of Dark Flash Fiction) by Pill Hill Press.

BY THE LIGHT OF THE MOON

The moon shone over the pumpkin patch, giving it an eerie glow. Pumpkins, all shapes and sizes, rested on the damp ground in the bright moonlight. The scarecrow, hanging from his stick backbone, loomed over the patch as if guarding it from harm. The dead cornstalks of the maze rustled in the cool breeze.

Bobby and Alex emerged from the corn maze where they had been hiding until the farm was closed for the day.

"Come on, Alex—let's do this!" Bobby ran to the patch and slammed his foot into a pumpkin. It broke into several pieces, guts spilling everywhere. Alex joined him, laughing as he also destroyed a pumpkin. The two boys ran around the patch, stomping on pumpkins, covering their jeans in seeds and sinew.

Several minutes later, Bobby realized he could no longer hear Alex. He turned around, looking for his friend. He cried out in terror as he saw the scarecrow holding Alex by the throat. The scarecrow grinned and twisted Alex's head sharply, breaking his neck. It dropped Alex into a pile of smashed pumpkins and then looked at Bobby. It beckoned to Bobby, with a crooked straw finger.

Bobby took off running, but tripped over a pumpkin vine and fell to the ground. He tried to get up, but could only roll over onto his back in pain. Suddenly the scarecrow was in front of him. Before Bobby could even scream, the scarecrow slammed its foot into Bobby's stomach, spilling guts everywhere.

Since February is Women in Horror Month, the contest focused on female characters. I didn't write as a mom this time; my character was a terrified but brave little girl.

RESCUE

Sadie screamed, beating her fists against metal. She had woken up in the dark trunk of a car.

The car stopped hard, and Sadie heard gunfire. *I won't let anybody hurt me!* Frantically she felt around for a weapon. Her hand grasped something metal and heavy; she held it close.

Suddenly the trunk opened. "It's OK, little girl—" Sadie quickly sat up and hit the man's head with a crowbar. He went down, blood and brain matter flying.

"No! No, little girl!" Another man grabbed the crowbar. Crying, Sadie looked down at the dead man in his policeman's uniform.

In April 2011, the theme was required words. Here is the list of words we had to use:

NOUNS: Bourbon, Jalapeno, Manatee, Skyscraper

VERBS: Belch, Saturate, Write, Yodel

ADJECTIVES: Buxom, Fingerlicking, Floral, Pastel

This was a fun contest. I wrote and submitted three stories — and all three stories were chosen. Since the stories are judged blind, nobody knew I wrote all three. This was a first for the Necon E-books contest, and a huge moment for me. My story "That Day" was chosen as a winner, and the other two "Blonds Have More Fun" and "A Day at the Sea Park" were included in the end-of-year anthology instead of published on the site, so that other authors could be featured as well.

THAT DAY

When the first skyscraper came down, Sam thought the world was coming to an end. When the second one fell with his wife inside, he was sure.

Now ten years later, he could finally write about that day for his new book. His heart was still broken, but he smiled when he pictured Christine leaving the house, gorgeous in her floral-patterned dress. She had left early as usual; Sam couldn't help think that she'd still be alive if only she had stayed in bed with him a little longer. She had gently rebuffed him, citing meetings and clients.

If only.

Blondes Have More Fun

The buxom blonde was well on her way to being drunk from the bourbon shots, courtesy of the guy at the end of the rooftop bar. He looked sleazy, but hey, free booze. Janet tossed back her fourth shot and slammed the glass down. The man sauntered up next to her.

"Hey, Baby," he purred. "Enjoying those drinks?"

Janet rolled her eyes. "I'll write about it in my diary tonight."

He followed Janet to the edge of the roof. "I'll give you something *else* to write about, Sugar."

"You just did," she said, as she pushed him over the side.

A Day at the Sea Park

The manatee drew big crowds, as did the killer whale. The front row loved it when Ramu would saturate them with seawater.

But a tragedy changed it all.

The investigation revealed that the rollercoaster was tampered with after inspection. The culprit was never found.

Bodies splattered to the ground; some landing in the aqua theater tank, the blood driving the killer whale into a frenzy and turning the water a pastel pink.

Crazed, the whale killed its trainer, pulling her down to the bottom of the tank. The audience ran screaming, horrified.

But one person stayed in his seat, smiling.

Dark Romance was the theme for June 2011. "Love stories gone horribly wrong," according to the guidelines, and that was something I enjoyed writing about. This story is an Honorable Mention winner, and was recently accepted as a reprint in the upcoming anthology ANOTHER 100 HORRORS.

IN DEEP

When Alex's fist connected with Lisa's jaw, she swore to herself that he'd pay. She grabbed the crystal ashtray and cracked the side of his head. He dropped like a stone.

Lisa admired her handiwork. Alex's legs were bound with a padlocked chain. His arms were behind his back, wrists shackled together with handcuffs once playfully used.

Alex realized he was lying at the bottom of their empty pool.

"You'll starve or drown; I don't care. Nobody will help you, Alex, just like nobody helped me."

She dropped the hose into the pool and walked away.

"See you in hell."

September 2011's contest theme was Autumn. For me, Autumn is the first day of school, a new year to stress over my kids' homework and extra-curricular activities. But this kind of beginning would be more terrifying.

FIRST DAY OF SCHOOL

Miss Greenwood smiled at the children sitting at their desks. "Good morning! I hope everyone had a wonderful summer."

Silence greeted her. Miss Greenwood's smile faltered and she brushed strands of hair off her shoulder. "Well! Anyway, I know we'll have another great year together."

Still nothing. Her voice wavered. "OK. It'll be OK." Tears ran down her gaunt cheeks. She gazed at the children.

They were in various stages of decay, some still sitting upright. Nuclear winds raged outside as Miss Greenwood fought desperately to keep what was left of her sanity.

Around this time, I was getting into book reviewing in a big way. I was reading for several small-press publications and review sites, and letting my own writing fall by the wayside. My next contest winner was in June of 2012, with the theme of Teenagers. Now THAT was something I could write about. This story was an Honorable Mention, and my last winning flash of 2012.

EVIDENCE: EXHIBIT A—EXCERPTS FROM JENNIFER TANEY'S DIARY

9/28/12

Mom really pissed me off tonight. As usual. And clean my room? Yeah, right. Clean it yourself.

10/5/12
So I'm failing Algebra. Big deal. Now I'm grounded. Bitch.

10/12/12
Why can't she leave me alone? She hates Jimmy because I love him. Says he's a bad influence and I can't see him anymore. I wish I could live by myself.

11/30/12
Thanksgiving sucked. She's such a bitch. If she'd just go away, it would make my Christmas.

12/25/12
I put Jimmy's bag of heroin in her smoothie this morning. She died pretty gross, but my Christmas wish came true.

THE SHORT STORIES

I got my first magazine acceptance in 1999 in a now-defunct magazine called The Midnight Gallery. It was edited by Jennifer Hardin, and I shared the Table of Contents with some great writers. It was the first time I had my name in print, and it was an amazing feeling. After reading this again to include here, I'm still pretty proud of this little story.

THE STORM PEOPLE

"Get away from that window! There's a storm brewing!"

Brian's grandfather struggled to push himself out of his favorite chair, turning red from the effort.

Brian didn't understand his grandfather's consternation. He and his family were staying at a rented beach house for the summer, and Brian was bored. His parents were out having lunch with a couple they had met on the beach, and Mandy, his younger sister, was taking a nap in her room. A good thunderstorm seemed just the thing to liven his day a bit.

"What's the problem, Gramps? I want to watch the lightning strike over the water. And the water is getting really choppy—look at all those whitecaps!" Just exciting enough for a young boy of fourteen.

"Haven't you ever heard of the Storm People, boy?" the old man asked in his smoking-induced raspy voice. He slowly sat back down in his chair, gripping the armrests to steady himself. Thinking he was about to endure another of his grandfather's rambling stories, Brian rolled his eyes and let out a heavy sigh. "No, Gramps. By why don't you tell me all about it?"

"Enough of your snippy tone! Sit down and listen to me.

The Storm People are evil spirits, boy; souls of those who have passed on, but aren't ready to enter the gates of Hell, where they belong. You can't see them on a sunny day, of course; evil prefers the dark. But when the storm clouds start to gather, that's when their time is nearing."

"Come on, Gramps! Do you really expect me to believe a story like that? Why are you telling me this now? Why weren't you upset when I watched the storms back home from the balcony?"

"We live in the city, in a high-rise apartment. The Storm People prefer to gather in the open. The beach is perfect for them. But they also gather in meadows, on farms; they gather anywhere there is a wide, open space."

"So if I look out the window, I'll see them? Cool!" Not believing a word of his grandfather's story, Brian ran to the window and started to draw back the curtain.

"NO! You don't understand the danger. Let me finish telling you about these evil creatures. Sit DOWN, boy." Gramps pointed his bony finger at the couch; his hand shaking from either fear or anger. Maybe both.

The youngster sat down, slowly exaggerating his movements to show such an old person couldn't intimidate him. "Gramps, please stop calling me 'boy.' My name is Brian. B-R-I-A-N." He said this with as much insolence as a 14-year-old boy can muster, hoping to irritate his grandfather as much as he himself was irritated. He was missing the storm! Brian felt the thunder shake the house and could see the strobe light effect of the lightning through the partly drawn curtains.

Gramps leaned forward towards Brian, and poked his finger into Brian's chest. Although a little milky from age, Gramps's eyes were still ice blue. Looking into his grandfather's steely gaze, Brian realized he had better start showing a little more respect for the old man. Otherwise, his dad might not let him watch the horror movie on TV that he was looking forward to that night.

"The Storm People are not ready to leave their Earthly existence. No, they have much work here on Earth, evil deeds they delight in. But they can't perform such acts in their spirit state. They need bodies, human bodies. And the only way they can get a body is if you make eye contact with one. The Storm People won't come looking for you, but if you were to look out that window and one of them saw you, your soul would be in mortal danger." Gramps sat back in his chair and lit his pipe, his hands still shaking.

"They're frolicking out there right now, Brian. They're running along the beach, looking at the houses, hoping for a glimpse of someone peeking out of a window. God help the person they see."

"How do you know about them, Gramps? Have you ever really seen them?" There was no sarcasm to Brian's tone now; Gramps's intensity was contagious, and he could see the old man was serious. Maybe there really was something to this story. Truthful story or not, though, it was starting to give Brian the creeps.

"Yes, I've seen 'em. I was just a little older than you are now. My own grampa had warned me about the Storm People, but like you, I didn't believe him. Thought he was just old and senile. But I wish I had listened to him then. Dear God, I wish I had listened." He took a puff off his pipe and realized it had gone out. As he relit it, Brian realized his grandfather's hands were shaking worse than before. It took a few tries to get the pipe going again.

"So what happened, Gramps? I'll listen to what you say—I promise." Brian's voice was just a little above a whisper, as if he were afraid the Storm People would hear him.

Gramps sighed. It was the sigh of a man who feels as if he has the weight of the world upon his shoulders. "I'll tell you, boy. I told this story to your daddy once, and he just laughed at me. Maybe you'll take heed of my words." He put his head back against the chair and closed his eyes.

"I was sixteen years old, and thought I knew it all. I was spending the summer at my grampa's farm, helping him tend the livestock. I had done that every summer since I was about 7 or 8 years old, and I had lots of friends over there. But my best friend was Danny Dixon. He and I were just about inseparable. You didn't see one of us without t'other."

A clap of thunder crashed directly over the house. Both Brian and his grandfather jumped. Brian hoped his sister wouldn't wake up from her nap. He was too interested in the story to deal with her. "Go on, Gramps—I'm listening."

"Well, there was one afternoon when Danny and I were supposed to go riding after we finished our chores. I had one beauty of a horse, and Danny and I loved to race against each other. A storm was brewing, though, and my grampa refused to let me go out. That's when he told me about the Storm People. Hell, like I said, I didn't believe him. So I left. He tried to come after me, but he was no match for a boy my age. I ran to the barn, got my horse and galloped over to Danny's house.

"By the time I got there, the rain had started and I could already hear thunder in the distance. Danny was already on his horse, waiting for me. We decided to take a quick ride through the field, then we'd put the horses in the barn and get a snack.

"We were having a wonderful time riding those horses, whooping and hollering loudly enough to wake the dead." Gramps tried to chuckle, but only managed a wheeze. "We didn't realize the dead were already awake."

Brian thought the story was interesting, but he still didn't think he believed everything Gramps was saying. He did want to hear the rest, though. "Come on, Gramps—tell me what happened!"

"Well, there we were, riding along and having a grand old time. The storm was practically on top of us, and we were getting soaked to the bone. That's what I saw them. The Storm People. They didn't look like real people, of course; they were just spirits. Even though they looked like they were wearing black cloaks and hoods, you could still kinda see through 'em. Couldn't see faces on 'em, either, but you could see eyes—red eyes. I was terrified, but I remembered my grampa telling me not to make eye contact. I jumped off my horse, and yelled at Danny to do the same. I fell to my knees, and kinda made a ball out of myself, covering my head with my arms and closing my eyes real tight. I kept screaming at Danny to follow my lead. The storm was so loud, though. I guess he never heard me."

Brian's eyes were wide and bright. "What happened,

Gramps? What happened to Danny? Did the Storm People get him?"

"Yeah, they got him. I stayed curled up in a ball until that storm passed. It was probably only about ten minutes, but it felt like hours. I was soaking wet and shivering with cold. And fear. When I stood up, Danny was still up on his horse, wet as I was. He wasn't shivering, though. He was just sitting up there, calm as could be. I asked him if he was OK, and when he turned to answer me, I saw."

"Saw what, Gramps? Saw what?" Brian sounded breathless, as if he had been the one in the storm.

"Saw Danny had been turned, boy! As he was twisting his body towards me, I saw a red tinge to his eyes. He said he was OK, but I knew better. He jumped off his horse and came towards me. He had a smile on his face, but it was a smile that made my skin crawl. I started backing up, telling him to get away from me. 'What's the matter?' he asked me. 'You're one of the Storm People now. Leave me alone!' I yelled at him. He told me I was being ridiculous, that he didn't even know who the Storm People were. But I knew he was lying. I wasn't sure what to do."

"Well, what did you do, Gramps? Did you run from him? Did you tell his mom what had happened?"

"No, boy. I didn't do any of those things. I killed him. Pulled out my pocketknife and stabbed him in the chest. They found him a few days later. The 'killer' was never found." Gramps sighed. "I didn't have any choice. He was evil and I couldn't let him get loose. Who knows what he would have done if given the chance! I just did what I had to do."

"But Gramps—how could you really know for sure Danny had become one of the Storm People? Just because you thought you saw some red in his eyes doesn't really mean anything. And the Storm People is probably just a story! My God, Gramps, you KILLED your best friend!" Brian couldn't believe it—his grandfather was a murderer!

"Believe in the Storm People or not, boy—I don't care. It was my duty to tell you about them, and told you I have. Yes, I killed Danny. But once one of the Storm People had gotten him, he wasn't Danny anymore anyway. I did him a favor.

"Go and get me a beer, boy. All this talking has worn me out. And mind you, now—don't look out the window!"

Brian walked through the swinging door into the kitchen. "My grandfather is a murderer, my grandfather is a murderer." Brian repeated these words to himself, hoping to make them sound ridiculous. He didn't want to believe what he had just been told.

He opened the refrigerator door and pulled out a beer for his grandfather and a Coke for himself. He closed the door and started towards the living room. The window above the sink caught his eye. Hesitantly, he walked towards it. "It's just a story," he told himself. "And I'm going to prove it right now!"

Brian put the cans on the counter and leaned over the sink to reach the window. He pulled the curtains back and looked out at the beach. He saw nothing except the whitecaps on the water. Even though it was afternoon, the storm had brought darkness early. As he was about to close the curtains, lightning lit up the sky. And there they were, just as Gramps had described them— the Storm People, looking as if they were wearing black cloaks and hoods. As if they had sensed Brian, the Storm People turned towards his house. Brian shut his eyes quickly and closed the curtains.

"It's true! And I could've become one of them! Gramps! Hey, Gramps!" Brian practically tripped over his own feet trying to get back to the living room. "Gramps, you were right! I didn't believe you, but I saw them!"

Brian burst through the swinging doors into the living room. At first he didn't understand what he was seeing. His little sister was holding a pillow over their grandfather's face. Gramps wasn't moving. As she looked up at Brian, she smiled. He could see the reddish tint to her eyes.

"Oh, Brian—I'm going to have so much fun!" She put her small hands to her mouth and giggled.

Back around 1999/2000, I joined an email group called hor-rorwriters. I met some great people on that list, and we are friends to this day—Monica O'Rourke, Tim Arsenault, Brian Knight, James Newman—the list goes on. I'm so grateful I signed up. We decided to put out an anthology called R.A.W. (Random Acts of Weirdness). I think it was a pretty cool little anthology. My story "Red Handed" was part of it.

RED HANDED

"So what's the verdict, Ray? Am I going to live?" Martin grinned at the doctor as he buttoned his shirt.

"Well, in spite of those extra pounds you're lugging around, your high blood pressure and an ulcer in the making, yeah, you'll live—for now." The doctor scribbled briefly on Martin's chart.

"Great, Doc, thanks. Still up for golf on Saturday morning?" Ray had been Martin's physician for the past fifteen years, his golfing buddy for nearly ten.

"Hold up, Martin. We're not through. You're only fifty-five years old, but you're not going to make it to sixty if you don't make some serious changes in your lifestyle."

"Christ, Ray, don't go all 'serious doctor' on me. Write me a prescription for the high blood pressure and even diet pills if you think it's really necessary. But come on, I can't be that bad off."

Ray shook his head. "Sorry, Martin, but it's not that simple. Yes, I'll give you a scrip to help lower your blood pressure. However, you'll need to do your part as well."

"What do you mean?" Here it comes, the diet and exercise spiel.

Ray smiled as if he could read his friend's thoughts. "You didn't get to this point overnight, Martin. Your biggest problem is stress. You keep everything bottled up inside. Sooner or later you're going to blow. Trust me, it won't be pretty."

"So what should I do? You have me a little nervous here."

"Good! Usually it takes my patients a mild heart attack before they take me seriously." The doctor leaned back against the stainless-steel counter and crossed his arms. "You need an outlet. Keep one of those squishy stress balls in your pocket. When your boss gives you shit, pretend the ball is his scrawny little neck and squeeze the hell out of it."

Martin raised his eyebrows. "You really think that will help? Frankly, it sounds ridiculous."

Ray chuckled. "That's just an example, Martin. You need to find what works for you. It could be exercise, meditation— anything that lessens your tension noticeably. Find it soon, my friend. You're a ticking time bomb, if you'll excuse the tired cliché."

A couple weeks later Martin was at his desk, pouring over ledgers that wouldn't make sense. If he didn't make the numbers reconcile, there'd be hell to pay. He already knew he'd have to work late again, something that was sure to piss Margie off. Martin mentally shrugged. Everything set her off these days. She was becoming a real goddamn shrew.

Martin was so engrossed in the task at hand that he jumped when the phone rang, snapping his pencil in two. "Shit, what now?" he griped, picking up the phone.

"Martin Simmons," he said, automatically assuming his professional demeanor.

"So what time are you going to tear yourself away from the place?"

Great. "And hello to you too, Margie. How's your day?" Martin was determined to keep the conversation pleasant.

"It's a shitty day, of course, just as I expected. Right now I'm home for lunch. I had to get out of there. I get so damn tired of disgusting runny noses, screaming babies, vomit, diarrhea—"

"Margie, nobody's stopping you from finding another job. It's pretty obvious you hate working there. Dr. Marshall can find another receptionist."

"Yeah, right. You know we need my insurance plan since yours sucks. I'm trapped here. I don't know why I decided to work for a pediatrician. Why didn't I pick a geriatric practice? At least they're mostly quiet. And anyway, why don't *you* start looking for another job? Something with decent pay and benefits, for Christ's sake ..."

Shit, here we go. Knowing anything he said would only encourage more complaining, Martin cradled the phone between his ear and shoulder and rummaged through the clutter of mail strewn about his desk. *Where is it, where is it? Ah-ha.* Martin found his stress ball and squeezed it, occasionally *"mmm-hmming"* dutifully when there was a lull in Margie's tirade. *This stupid ball sucks,* he thought, and threw it across the office.

Martin grabbed the silver-plated letter opener his cheapskate boss had given him for Christmas the year before and ripped open the first of many envelopes he needed to wade through that afternoon. Absorbed in this task, he mumbled "Yes, dear" at an inappropriate time.

"God *damn* it, Martin!" his wife shrieked. Startled, Martin accidentally sliced the soft pad of his thumb on the sharp point of the letter opener. "You're not even listening to me!" Margie continued, her rage now in full bloom. "I swear, I don't know why I even bother ..."

Margie's shrill voice faded to a dull, faraway noise, like the drone of a distant honeybee. Martin couldn't take his eyes off the thin line of blood welling up from the wound on his thumb. Fascinated, he watched the blood drip slowly onto his desk blotter. Martin sat back in his imitation-leather chair and closed his eyes. The tension escaped his body rapidly; it was almost as good as an orgasm.

"Oh, yeahhhhhhhhh," Martin groaned softly.

"Well, I'm glad we agree on *something* for a change," Margie replied peevishly, rudely jolting Martin back to the here-and-now. "So what should we do about it?"

Of course he had absolutely no clue what his wife was babbling about. He wasn't about to let her know that, though.

"Why don't we discuss it tonight, honey?" He was amazed at how good he felt. "I'll even pick up some dinner on the way home."

There was a slight pause on Margie's end. Martin knew the "honey" had thrown her. "Um ... that sounds good. See you around seven?"

Martin heard the confusion in her voice and chuckled inwardly. "You betcha. Bye, Margie." He hung up the phone and went back to his numbers, feeling calm and relaxed for the first time in years.

Later, as he left the office, he picked up the stress ball and tossed it into his trashcan.

The euphoria lasted almost a week. He and Margie got along better than they had in months. They even made love on Wednesday—typically this perfunctory task was performed on the occasional Saturday night if there was nothing worth watching on HBO. Usually there was.

"I swear, Martin—you've been in such a good mood lately. It's like I've been living with a different man the past few days!" Margie snuggled closer to her husband, sated from having sex for the second time in a week.

"Yeah, well. Work's been going pretty good this week." Martin glanced at the alarm clock on the nightstand. The sex had been okay, but he just wasn't up for cuddling and making pillow talk.

"Martin!" Margie sat up fast, the covers falling from her body. Her doughy breasts flopped against her chest and she crossed her arms tightly against them. "Did you just look at the clock?"

"Margie—"

"Am I *boring* you, Martin? You got fucked, now you've got *better* things to do?" Her voice rose dangerously. Her cheeks burned red and her eyes glistened wetly. "You bastard. Get out. Go sleep on the couch."

"Margie, come on. I'm sorry, okay?" Martin was not in the mood for a fight. His stomach twisted itself into knots.

"I said get *OUT!*" Margie grabbed her pillow and slammed it into Martin's face.

Martin got out of bed and stared down at his wife. "Christ, Margie. Sometimes you can be a real cunt." He picked up his boxers and walked out the bedroom. His head throbbed with the echo of his wife's sobs.

Martin tossed and turned on the couch, fuming over their argument. What a whiny bitch. Who the hell does she think she is, whacking me with the pillow like that? All I did was check the time!

Finally he sat up and reached for the remote on the coffee table. Mindlessly he surfed the TV, stomach acid churning in his belly and traveling up his throat. "Damn it!" Martin stalked into the kitchen and yanked open the refrigerator door. He grabbed a Coors Light and twisted off the cap, then took a long swallow of the icy-cold beer. He rubbed the cap between his thumb and forefinger, eyeing it thoughtfully. Martin put the bottle on the counter, then slowly, savoring the feeling, drew the sharp edge of the cap down the length of his palm. The pain was exquisite.

"Oh, yes. Oh, *fuck* yes." Martin's knees buckled and his cock hardened uncomfortably. Blood flowed from the cut on his hand. He pushed his boxers down to his ankles and started jerking off with his injured hand. Blood smeared his cock and dripped on the floor. Martin braced himself against the counter with his free hand, his balls slapping up against the silverware drawer. He came in less than a minute, biting his tongue hard so he wouldn't scream. His semen spurted all over Margie's ceramic flour and tea canisters and oozed onto the Formica countertops. Sweat poured down his face and his legs shook, but Martin barely noticed.

Exhausted but euphoric, Martin cleaned up the kitchen and bandaged his hand. Then he headed upstairs to make up with his wife.

Martin took to keeping a small supply of X-Acto knives with

him at all times. Whenever he felt the stress building up, he would subtly cut himself. The ensuing rush enabled Martin to cope with the tension. He also carried a stock of adhesive bandages in his wallet. It didn't take Margie long to notice the bandages on his fingers.

"What have you been doing to yourself, Martin?" She grabbed his wrist and shook it, smacking his fingers together. The tiny slits under the bandages tingled at the rough motion. Martin's cock twitched in response.

He snatched his hand back. "I've just been getting lots of paper cuts lately. So much paperwork to sort through these days. Don't worry."

"You're so clumsy, Martin. And you look ridiculous with those Band-Aids wrapped around your fingers." She laughed and rolled her eyes at him. Martin wondered how it would feel to stick an X-acto knife in one of those eyes. He stomped off to the bathroom, her cruel laughter following close behind.

He slammed the door and locked it. He yanked down his jeans and whipped out one of his knives.

This time, he cut his leg.

"I'm sorry, Martin. I wish it didn't have to be this way." Mr. Wilkerson's voice dripped with insincerity.

Martin's hands were clenched tightly by his thighs, the knuckles dead white. "But I've worked for this company for over ten years! I'm one of the best accountants you've got—you know that!"

Martin's boss sighed and leaned back in his black leather chair. "You're also one of the most expensive, Martin. You of all people should know how hard this company is struggling to stay afloat. I've got to cut costs where I can."

"Maybe you should lose the whore you keep in that fancy apartment," Martin muttered under his breath.

"I'm sorry, what did you say?" The question was mild, but Martin heard the sinister undertone. He knew he'd better shut up if he wanted his pitiful severance package.

"Nothing. I'll go clear out my desk." He stood up and walked to the door.

"Martin, wait—"

His heart leapt hopefully at Wilkerson's words, and he turned, ready to forgive his boss and accept the offer of his job back.

Wilkerson's smile couldn't hide the spite in his eyes. "Make sure you turn in your keys."

Martin slammed the door behind him.

Martin sat on the toilet in the men's room a few minutes later, desperately jabbing at his thigh with one of his knives. Blood dripped onto the tile floor, but euphoria eluded Martin this time. What the hell was he going to tell Margie?

The knife clattered to the floor as Martin buried his face in his hands and sobbed.

"What the hell do you mean, you were fired? What the *fuck* are we going to do now? See, I told you I couldn't quit my crappy job! I'm going to rot there, Martin, *rot* in that goddamn hellhole. All because you're a loser who can't support his wife."

"Margie, please calm down. I can get another job." He wished he could curl up into the fetal position but wouldn't give the shrew the satisfaction. Instead he leaned back in his recliner and closed his eyes. His leg throbbed where he had cut it earlier. His cock, however, hung limply in his pants. *What can I do to get the feeling back? I'll have a fucking stroke if I don't!*

"You stupid jerk! You're not even listening to me! Look at you, lying in that chair like a lazy dog. I don't know why I ever married you. My life is *shit* thanks to you!"

Martin reluctantly opened his eyes and beheld his once-beautiful bride perched on the couch. Her eyes blazed with disgust and hatred, her mouth a thin angry line. Martin's heart pounded painfully in his chest, and he thought about his doctor's warning. *I've got to do something.* He looked longingly at his briefcase sitting on the dining room table, wishing he could get a knife out of it.

"Pay attention to me!" Margie screamed. "That's your whole problem, Martin—you're always lost in some dream world. No wonder you never amounted to anything!" Margie's graying hair flew about wildly as she carried on, reminding Martin of a fat Medusa. He shuddered, repulsed.

"I can't do this anymore." Martin stood up suddenly, his heart racing and the blood rushing to his brain.

"I'm not finished with you yet! Sit down right now, Martin!" Now she looked like a troll, squat and piggish.

"Fuck you, Margie." Martin headed for the kitchen, leaving his wife staring at him in disbelief.

He rummaged through the silverware drawer, but couldn't find exactly what he knew he needed. Cutlery landed on the floor, clinking on the linoleum. At this point, a mere kitchen knife wouldn't give him the release he so urgently needed.

"Goddamn it, Martin! What are you doing in there?"

At this sound of his wife's voice, Martin's chest heaved as he tried to catch his breath. He grabbed a glass from the cupboard and turned on the faucet. He heard the couch squeak, which meant Margie had gotten up and was coming to see what he was fucking up to this time. Frantically he looked around the kitchen for something that would give him quick release.

Then he looked at the sink and smiled with relief.

Margie walked into the kitchen just as Martin flipped the switch to the garbage disposal, his arm wedged into the drain.

Blood spouted while bits of flesh and bone spattered about the kitchen. Martin's head was thrown back and his whole body twitched and jittered. The front of his slacks was soaked with semen.

His screams of ecstasy were indistinguishable from Margie's screams of fear and disgust.

My second magazine acceptance was a little magazine called Darkness Within, edited by G. Durant Haire. My story appeared in the third issue, in Winter 2000. Once again, I shared the Table of Contents with some wonderful writers, including D.F. Lewis and Carlton Mellick III. The great artist Allen Koszowski created the beautiful cover art. My story, "Spider Bites," gave me the willies writing it.

SPIDER BITES

WHAP! The newspaper in Marty's hand smashed the black, hairy spider in its tracks as it skittered across the dingy kitchen tile.

A shudder rushed up Marty's spine as he bent down to scoop up the offending creature into the newspaper. Bloody flat spider bits smeared across the floor. Marty could feel his corn-flakes making a rapid return and rushed across the room to the kitchen sink. He let them go, splattering the dishes from last night's dinner.

What a shitty day this is starting out to be, he thought, sending the used cornflakes down the drain with scalding hot water.

Marty Brennan loathed spiders, considered them an abomination. Kate, his bitch-from-hell wife—*ex-wife,* Marty though gleefully—thought they were cool. She'd never let him kill any that he found in the condo; she'd always pick them up gently and take them outside. Sometimes, she would actually bring one in from outside to show Marty just how "cute" the fucking thing was. Kate's fascination with spiders was just one of many reasons Marty was glad to be rid of her.

He walked through the small apartment to the closet-sized bathroom, needing to replace the sour cornflake taste with minty-fresh breath. He decided to worry about the dead spider later. He had more important things to deal with first.

Like how to get rid of Kate's body.

Teeth cleaned and hair combed, Marty emerged from the bathroom a few minutes later, feeling much better. But he still had a problem. Two actually, if he counted the squashed spider on the kitchen floor. He chose to deal with the dead wife first. Easier on his frayed nerves.

Marty didn't mean to kill Kate. It was her fault, really. She knew he hated spiders, but she must've lost her mind for a moment because she actually put one of the fuckers on his shoulder.

She sure as hell didn't expect the reaction he gave her. That part was Marty's fault, though. Maybe he should've told Kate that it was more than dislike he felt for spiders; he was downright terrified of them. Marty had never shared with Kate the time he had been locked in a shed by some assholes when he was a kid. The place was dark and crawling with spiders. By the time his big brother had rescued him, Marty was nearly catatonic. For months afterward, he would get the horrible sensation that spiders were crawling on him. Sometimes he'd wake up at night screaming, convinced he was covered with them. Had Kate known, she probably wouldn't have played her little joke. Or maybe she would've. Sometime Kate could be such an evil bitch.

Marty walked into the bedroom where Kate was still sprawled on the floor, her eyes staring unseeingly at the ceiling. She looked as if she were mesmerized by the glow-in-the-dark solar system they had once stuck up there on a whim. Back when they spent a lot of their time together in bed.

The pool of blood under Kate's head had congealed to a gooey, paint-like consistency. Her lily-white skin had taken on a bluish tinge, as if she were freezing cold. Which, Marty supposed with a snicker, she was.

He felt no guilt for his part in Kate's death. He didn't intend to kill her; pushing her down was just a reaction to the terror and anger he felt at her stupid prank. It was unfortunate she happened to slam the back of her head on the sharp corner of the bureau as she went down. Really, she brought it on herself.

Marty went into the living room and grabbed the hideous purple and red Oriental rug Kate had insisted on buying a few months ago. Well, now he could finally be rid of them both.

He dragged the offensive rug into the bedroom and laid it out on the bed. He looked over at Kate and grinned. "Well, I guess this is it. Time for you to move on, Darlin'." He put his arms underneath her and started to lift her up. He felt a sharp pain in the palm of his right hand. Marty yanked his hands out from underneath Kate's body and screamed in pain and terror.

A white spider about the size of a half-dollar sat in the middle of his hand, its tiny fangs still embedded in Marty's flesh. The same goddamned spider Kate had put on his shoulder. Marty had wondered where the thing had gone after he had flicked it off his shoulder.

He gave a forceful shake of his hand, sending the monstrous creature flying across the room. The spider smacked into the wall and slid to the floor.

Marty scooted frantically over to the bed on his butt and leaned back against it, breathing hard and fast. His hand was throbbing painfully in rhythm with his heartbeat. "You stupid bitch! You had to bring that goddamn spider into our home!" Marty thrust his leg out and gave Kate's body a savage kick. He wished she could feel it.

The stinging in his hand brought his attention back to the spider bite. Marty looked at his palm, frightened and sickened at what he saw there.

A viscous white fluid oozed out of the swollen punctures, leaving a sticky, slug-like trail. Small black specks peppered the sappy fluid.

Marty wiped his palm on his shirt. The goo clung to his hand as he pulled it away, stretching like snot after a violent sneeze.

"Jesus, what *is* this shit?"

Before he could even begin to figure out what was going

on, a movement across the room caught his eye. The spider was coming back at him, hauling ass across the hardwood floor. Marty had never seen a spider crawl so fast. The damn thing was practically galloping! The sight paralyzed him with fear. All he could do was scream helplessly as the spider made its way up his left leg under his faded blue denim jeans.

The pain as the creature sank its fangs into the meat of his leg was worse than the pain in his hand. He felt the slimy fluid ooze slowly down his leg. Marty frantically pounded his fist against the spider lump under his pants, feeling it burst and flatten on his leg.

Nearly insane with terror by this time, Marty scrambled to his feet and tried to yank his jeans off.

"Fuck, fuck, FUCK!" Marty screamed hysterically. He finally remembered he had to unbuckle his belt first. With shaking hands he quickly undid the Budweiser belt buckle. He fumbled with the button fly for a few nightmarish seconds, then finally yanked the jeans down, alternately hopping on one foot as he pulled off each pant leg.

Most of the squashed spider remained in the discarded jeans, but there were a few spider pieces clinging to the hairs on his leg. The white slime was also smeared on his leg; countless black specks were scattered throughout it, just like in his hand.

"Need a shower, need a shower," he mumbled incoherently. Exhausted from his harrowing ordeal, Marty sank to the floor. A quick glance at the clock radio on the nightstand told him only a few minutes had passed since the spider attacked him, although it seemed like hours. Marty leaned back against the bed again and closed his eyes, breathing heavily.

He had actually started to doze when he felt as if his hand and leg were being pierced with dozens of razor-sharp needles.

Marty's eyes flew open and he cried out in pain. The cries became shrieks of pure terror when he saw what was happening.

The peppery specks were breaking open—*hatching, dear god they're hatching,* his mind gibbered—each one releasing a tiny midnight-black spider. The bites these tiny monsters inflicted upon him were much more painful than the original spider's; Marty felt as if his skin were on fire.

He smacked his hands together, trying to kill the spiders hatching on his palm. He only succeeded in transferring some of the spiders to the unbitten hand. The creatures immediately went to work on that hand. Thin rivulets of blood snaked down his arms and dropped to the floor.

Marty was no longer screaming; he had completely lost his voice. Only a harsh wheeze escaped his throat.

The pain in his leg became sheer agony. Spiders completely covered the lower part of his leg beneath the knee, a living blanket that rippled and undulated. The swarm slowly moved up his leg, leaving behind only bone and shredded flesh.

The spiders were eating Marty alive.

Without thinking, only reacting in mind-numbing horror, Marty covered his face with his hands and tried to scream. As if in a feeding frenzy, the spiders ate through his hands and skittered down his throat.

Marty had one final inane thought before what remained of his sanity blessedly checked out.

At least now he wouldn't have to deal with the dead spider in the kitchen.

The year 2000 was a good year for my writing. Another publication, Redsine, accepted my story "The Phone Call" for their second issue in May. I was published alongside some great writers—David Whitman, John Urbancik, and Brian Knight, just to name a few.

THE PHONE CALL

"Carrie? It's Paul." The voice on the telephone sounded hesitant, unsure.

"Hello, Paul. How are you?" Carrie's voice was calm, but her heart was pounding and her palms sweaty. She hadn't heard from her brother in almost ten years.

"Look, I wouldn't blame you if you hung up on me. You have every right. But I hope you won't."

"I won't hang up, Paul," Carrie said gently. "I'm glad you called, although I admit I'm surprised. What made you call me today?"

"This is going to sound sappy and clichéd, but it's Thanksgiving. What better time to make up? There's something I need to say that I should've said a long time ago. It won't take long; I'm sure you and Andrew have plans—"

"Andrew died two years ago, Paul. I have no plans."

Silence. Then—"Christ, Carrie, I am so sorry. What happened?"

Carried sighed, tears welling in her eyes. "I can't talk about it with you, Paul. It's too painful and personal."

"I remember when you talked to me about everything," Paul said sadly.

"So do I," Carrie retorted sharply. "But you put an end to that, didn't you?" The bitterness she felt toward her only sibling was still strong.

"That's why I'm calling, Carrie. I just want to say how sorry I am for the way I treated you back then. I know you only did what you thought was right. Even if I didn't agree with your decision, I should've supported you. What I did was reprehensible. I hope you can forgive me."

Carrie was stunned. She had prayed for this day, but never really expected it. "Do you really mean it, Paul?"

"Yes, I've missed you so much. It's been ten years—we've lost so much time already."

The weight of resentment and bitterness was removed from Carrie's shoulders instantly. She felt like floating.

"Oh, Paul! Thank you! Thank you!" She didn't try to hide the face she was crying; after all, Paul was crying as well.

They talked for almost two hours, catching up on each other's life. "Let's get together soon, Carrie. Can you come for Christmas?"

"I wouldn't miss it. I can't wait to see you."

They exchanged phone numbers, Carrie writing Paul's on the pad beside her bed. Reluctantly they said their good-byes, promising to talk again in a day or two.

After she hung up the phone, Carrie took her journal out of her nightstand. She recorded the conversation with her brother, while it was still fresh in her mind. She hadn't been this happy in a long time.

She fell asleep with a contented smile on her face.

The disembodied voice on the telephone sounded grim and official. "Mrs. Miller? Mrs. Carrie Miller?"

A wave of dread washed over her. "Yes, this is she. May I help you?"

"Mrs. Miller, I'm Lieutenant Wilson of the Chicago Police Department. I'm sorry to have to inform you that your brother Paul was killed in a car accident yesterday morning. It wasn't his fault, Ma'am. He was hit by a drunk driver and killed instantly."

With a sigh of relief, Carrie informed the policeman that

it couldn't have been her brother in the accident. She had just talked to Paul the night before.

"I'm sorry, Mrs. Miller. There is no mistake. The accident occurred yesterday morning at 4:30 am. Your brother's neighbor positively identified him. We found your name and number among his personal effects. His wife told us who you were and asked us to call you. I'm so sorry to have to tell you this, especially on Thanksgiving Day."

"What? But yesterday was Thanksgiving!" Carrie was thoroughly confused. "Is this a joke? What the hell is going on?"

"Um, Mrs. Miller? Maybe you should call someone to come and stay with you for a while. I'm sure this is all quite a shock. Would you like me to call someone for you?"

"No. No, thank you, Officer. I'll be all right." Carrie hung up the phone, reeling from the conversation.

It has to be a mistake. I just talked to Paul less than twelve hours ago! Carrie grabbed the notepad with Paul's phone number on it and dialed the number frantically.

"Hello?" A woman's voice, sounding sad and exhausted.

"Is Paul there?" Carrie blurted. "Please—I need to speak with him."

"Carrie? Is that you?"

"Donna? What's going on?" She hadn't talked to her sister-in-law in so long, but she recognized the voice immediately.

"Oh, Carrie! Paul was killed yesterday morning! Some asshole driving drunk hit his car head-on! What am I going to do without him?" Donna broke down into uncontrollable sobs.

"No! No, I just talked to him a few hours ago! He apologized to me—he wanted us to be a family again!"

As if Carrie hadn't just spoken, Donna continued, barely able to choke out the words. "He had been talking about calling you, Carrie. He missed you so much and felt lousy for what he had done to you. I wish he had had the chance to talk to you before he died. I'm sorry, Carrie. I can't talk anymore." Donna hung up the phone before Carrie could respond.

Carrie lay back against the pillows, emotionally drained. She put her head in her hands and cried, wishing she could get back all the years they had wasted. After her tears were spent and her hands were damp, Carrie started to smile. No matter what anybody said, she knew she and her brother had talked the night before. She would treasure that conversation for the rest of her life.

The disembodied voice on the telephone sounded grim and official. "Mr. Davidson? Mr. Paul Davidson?"

A wave of dread washed over him. "Yes, this is he. May I help you?"

"Mr. Davidson, I'm Lieutenant Parks of the Los Angeles Police Department. I'm sorry to have to inform you that your sister Carrie was found dead in her apartment this morning." The policeman hesitated. "Apparently she had been dead for several days. We're not sure yet as to the cause of death. A friend of your sister's found her when she stopped by to see your sister. You were listed as her next-of-kin. I'm so sorry to have to tell you this, especially on Thanksgiving Day."

"Thank you, Lieutenant," Paul said faintly. He hung up the phone and turned to Donna. "Carrie's dead."

"Oh, Paul—I'm so sorry." His wife hugged him fiercely. "Are you OK?"

"I was going to call her today—apologize for what an asshole I was to her. And now I'll never have the chance. I waited too long. Damn it, I waited too long!" Paul started sobbing into his wife's shoulder.

"Sshhh, it's OK. It'll be OK." Donna rocked him gently, and stroked his hair.

"It won't be OK. My sister died thinking her only brother hated her. I'll have to live with that the rest of my life. I'll never be able to forgive myself."

Donna continued rocking her husband, wishing she could make everything all right.

In 2002, a favorite writer of mine, Edo van Belkom, announced he was editing an anthology geared at teenagers, and the theme was teen fears, but written as horror stories. I wrote this story about anorexia, and to my delight and astonishment, he accepted it after suggesting a few edits. This was my first paid story, and it was a professional publication. I'm still very proud of it.

WASTING AWAY

Stacy lifted the fork to her mouth and carefully drew the piece of steak inside, trying not to let her lips touch the stainless-steel tines. She chewed the meat three times, careful not to swallow, then she spat the mangled piece of meat into her paper napkin as she wiped her lips. All the flavor—none of the calories. Stacy had the routine down to an art.

She ate some of the peas and a little bit of salad, but she politely declined the mashed potatoes and rolls her mother tried to foist on her, saying, "You eat like a bird, Stacy. You're nothing but skin and bones!" Luckily, her mother, exhausted as usual from working double shifts at the restaurant, would stare off into space while she ate and never noticed when Stacy spit out her food.

She would always take her own plate to the kitchen and scrape her meal into the garbage disposal. Then she would head up to her bathroom and weigh herself. If she was even half an ounce over ninety-five pounds, Stacy would either make herself vomit or pop a couple of the laxatives she kept taped to the back of the toilet.

She simply refused to get fat.

Tonight was a good night, though. The red LED readout on the bathroom scale showed a satisfying ninety-two pounds. Perhaps tomorrow morning, Stacy would splurge and have a piece of dry toast with her usual cup of black coffee.

She headed to her bathroom to perform the last part of her evening ritual. She stripped naked and stood in front of her full-length mirror. Not bad, she thought as she admired her skeletal figure. But you can look better than that. Skip the toast tomorrow morning. Obviously you've been eating too much. They'll have to wheel you to school on a dolly at this rate.

She wrapped herself in her robe and got busy with her homework.

The next morning, Stacy got up and did her exercises before showering. The morning ritual had begun. Next stop was the scale. Today she weighed ninety-three pounds. God, what a pig! No breakfast *or* lunch for me today! I'm such a whale. Disgusted with herself, she hopped in the shower, enjoying the hot spray on water on her always-cold body.

"Here you go, sweetie," said Stacy's mom as Stacy entered the kitchen. "Cinnamon-apple pancakes, your favorite." She turned to smile at her daughter, but the smile faltered when she saw Stacy's appearance. Her jeans were practically slipping off her hips, and sharp ribs poked through her T-shirt. Stacy's hair, once thick and luxuriant, lay limply on her shoulders. Her skin was sallow, having lost its youthful, peachy sheen.

"No thanks, Mom. I need to get to school. I'll just grab a cup of coffee and drink it on the way."

"Stacy, please! Eat something before you go. You're so *thin*. You're wasting away to nothing right before my eyes." She sniffed back her tears, aware that her crying would only make her daughter angry.

Stacy rolled her eyes and chose a travel mug from the cupboard. "You're so dramatic, Mom." She poured the hot, black coffee into the cup and sipped it gratefully. "I'm not *that* thin. And I really need to be extra careful—I gained a pound overnight. A whole pound! I don't want to end up like that butterball Margie. She can barely bend over to tie her own shoes!"

Stacy's mom wanted to grab her daughter by the shoulders and shake some sense into her. Her little girl was trying to starve herself, and she had no idea how to stop it. Not even their family doctor had been able to help. He'd just told her that all the girls wanted to be thin these days and suggested she give Stacy a multi-vitamin.

Tears ran down her face as she watched Stacy go off to school.

Stacy's lunchtime routine wasn't as difficult as breakfast and dinner. All of her friends were dieting—she was just best at it. She bought a bottle of water and a small salad before sitting down with her friends at their regular table.

"Have you seen Bruce lately? I think he's been working out—he looks so hunky!" Allison gestured to a blond boy in a Dallas Cowboys T-shirt across the room.

"I've had a crush on him for months," Stacy confided. "I'm hoping he'll ask me to the Winter Dance this year." Stacy blushed and took a small bite of lettuce. The group of fifteen-year-old girls dissolved into delighted giggles.

Except for one.

"He's cute and all, but there's no way I'd want to go out with him," said Tammy. Stacy turned to her, wondering why the girl always had to be so negative.

"Why not? What's wrong with him?" Stacy took a sip of her water and waited for Tammy's answer, knowing that whatever it was, it would irritate her.

"Someone who looks like Bruce wouldn't want to go out with a girl who didn't look as hot as he does. Who needs that kind of pressure? I don't want to worry about every ounce of food that goes into my mouth." Tammy shrugged and took a bite of her veggie burger.

Stacy looked over at Bruce, who was talking and laughing with other football players. His arms were strong and muscular, his shoulders broad. Stacy knew that underneath his shirt, he probably had a washboard stomach. Not an ounce of fat on him. He'd never want to go out with an oinker like her.

Miserably, she pushed her salad aside.

When Stacy got home from school, she noticed a plate of chocolate chip cookies on the kitchen table with a note that said "Love, Mom." She sighed angrily. Why doesn't she just give it a rest? How fat does she want to make me? Aren't I fat enough already?

She bypassed the cookies—They do smell good, though. If only they didn't have so many calories!—and opened the refrigerator for a bottle of water instead. As her hand touched the door handle, she gasped. She could clearly see the blue veins of her hand through the skin. Stacy slammed the refrigerator door and ran up to her room.

Standing naked in front of the mirror, she was fascinated with what she saw. Her skin was translucent, not just on her hand but over her entire body. She could see the veins and arteries branching out from her heart and snaking their way through her body like tendrils. It was just like one of the pictures in her biology book, only this was flesh and blood. *Her* flesh and blood. Her mom wouldabsolutely freak if she saw this.

Dinner that night was a strained and quiet affair. Her mom glanced sadly at the plate of cookies still on the table. Stacy moved the food around her plate and occasionally chewed a piece of chicken before spitting it into her napkin. Suddenly, she noticed that her mother was watching this ritual with a horrified look on her face.

"Dear God, Stacy! Is *this* what you've been doing? Spitting out your food? No wonder you're wasting away to nothing! You've got to eat!"

"Oh Mom, you're so dramatic! Relax! That was just a fatty piece of chicken, that's all. It was gross, so I spit it out."

Stacy's mom slammed her hand on the table, making her daughter jump. "Don't you lie to me, Stacy! Look at you— nothing but skin and bones! You're practically fading away in front of my eyes. I don't care what the doctor said. We're going to the hospital right now."

She pushed back her chair, knocking it over. Ignoring it,

she walked around the table and grabbed Stacy's wrist, but it slipped through her grasp, leaving smudges of makeup behind.

"What is this? Why are you wearing makeup on your hands?" She snatched a napkin off the table and wiped at Stacy's long, bony fingers, screaming at what she saw.

"Mom, please! Would you just relax? You're being ridiculous."

"We need to get you to the hospital right this instant, Stacy! You're sick ... very, very sick!"

"I'm fine. Just leave me alone." Stacy got up and pushed past her mother, desperately wanting to get to her room. Her mother ran after her, but Stacy got to her room first and locked the door. She stripped off her clothes and looked in the mirror again. Now she could see most of her bones through her skin.

"Stacy, let me in! Let me help you!" Her mother rattled the knob and banged on the door.

"Go away! I'm fine!" Stacy preened in front of the mirror, liking what she saw. Maybe Bruce would ask her out after all. He'd be able to see for himself that her body was free of any disgusting fat.

Stacy turned at the sound of a key in the lock. Her mother burst into the room, her hands flying to her mouth in terror.

"Oh my God! Stacy, you're ... you're transparent! You look like a ghost!" She ran to hug her daughter, but her arms went right through Stacy's body.

"Mom?" Stacy's voice trembled and a tear ran down her cheek. This was no longer cool—now it was just scary. "What's happening to me? I feel really funny!" She put her hands up in front of her face and watched in disbelief as they slowly disappeared.

Stacy's mom could do nothing but stand by helplessly and watch her only daughter fade away to nothing.

Also in 2002, I had a story accepted by Monica O'Rourke to the erotic horror anthology, Decadence 2. Again, I was included with amazing authors such as Nancy Kilpatrick, Ed Lee, and John Everson.

ASHES TO ASHES

"It was a beautiful service, dear. Greg would have loved it." Tanya gaped at the old woman and held back a sarcastic reply. But she knew Greg's great-aunt meant well. Platitudes were spouted when people died; nobody ever knew the right thing to say.

Tanya realized Aunt Abigail was waiting for a response. She forced a wan smile and patted the old lady's hand. "Thank you, Auntie."

She tried to make her escape, but Abigail grabbed her arm.

"Why won't you bury my nephew properly? I hear you're going to *burn* him." The old lady stared accusingly at her through rheumy eyes.

Christ. Tanya had already been through this with her mother-in-law. Thankfully, Greg had written the cremation into his will when they realized he wouldn't go into remission after the last round of treatments.

"It's what Greg wanted, Auntie. Oh, excuse me. There's someone I must talk to." Tanya quickly walked away before Auntie could say anything else. She just didn't have the strength for it. She wanted to go home and cry.

These people never liked me. I don't want to share my grief with them.

Tanya decided to say her good-byes and leave. She'd never see Greg's family again anyway.

Her footsteps echoed through the empty house. Walking in the front door was different this time. When Greg was in the hospital for his regular treatments, she knew he would be coming back home. Now, however, their cozy little house seemed cold and foreign in its emptiness.

Tears welled when she entered their bedroom. The bed was messy; she hadn't had the time or energy to make it since Greg's death.

She curled up on the bed and hugged Greg's pillow tightly against her body. She could still smell his scent in the sheets and pillowcase. She cried herself to sleep.

Several days later, she decided to put the urn in the bedroom. It sat on her nightstand next to a picture of Greg before he got so sick. Tanya found herself talking to the urn before she went to sleep at night.

"Maybe I'm going crazy, Greg. Talking to you like this. But God, I miss you so much." Tanya choked on the words as she tried to hold in a sob. "I want to make love with you and be held in your arms."

With a heavy sigh, she undressed and slipped beneath the sheets. She still couldn't bear to change them. Greg's lingering scent in the cool cotton against her skin provided a bit of comfort.

Tanya lay there in the dark, thinking of the last time she and Greg had made love. They both knew Greg didn't have much time left, and the sex was tender and bittersweet. They cried when it was over. The next day, Greg made his final trip to the hospital.

Tanya could feel the wetness between her thighs. The thought of making love with Greg had aroused her, and she ached for release. She reached down under the covers and began fingering her clit. She gasped at the waves of pleasure that raced through her body. Her orgasm was quick and strong, and she yelled out at its intensity.

Then the emptiness came rushing back.

She trudged through her days, only going through the motions at work. Her coworkers gave up trying to invite her to lunch or happy hour. Tanya always refused or just stared into space without acknowledging she'd heard the invitation.

"Tanya, are you OK, really?" her boss asked. He had invited Tanya into his office to talk.

She heard the genuine concert in Jerry's voice and fought back tears. "I'm all right." She offered a slight smile and wiped away a tear.

Jerry got up and sat on the edge of his desk in front of her. "Look, Tanya. I think you should take some time off. You're obviously still very distressed and rightfully so. Frankly, I'm surprised you came back as soon as you did."

She shrugged. "I guess I thought keeping busy would help. I'm sorry my work has been so poor lately."

Jerry dismissed her chagrin with a wave of his hand. "Don't even worry about it. Take a couple weeks or so—a month, if you need to. You've been through hell."

Tanya stood up and smiled gratefully. "Thank you so much. I really appreciate this." She reached out and shook his hand, then left quickly so she wouldn't cry in front of him.

"It's not getting any better, Greg." Tanya took a sip of Scotch from the bottle on the nightstand. The sheets were beginning to smell sour, but Tanya still couldn't bring herself to change them.

"I miss you so much. I *want* you so much. I'm ovulating— remember how badly we wanted a baby? I'm so wet and so horny, and I need you so badly." Tanya took a drag of her cigarette, then put it in the ashtray on the bed next to her.

She grabbed the Scotch and took a long pull. Some of the amber liquid leaked from the bottle and dripped onto her breasts. She traced the wet trail with her finger.

"You would lick that off if you were here. Remember I'd pour Scotch on your cock and suck it off? God, you loved that."

Tanya took another drink, then poured some of the alcohol over her body, splashing the bed. She rubbed the warm liquid into her body. She arched her back, letting the small pool on her stomach run in slow rivulets down to her pussy.

"I wish I could feel you against my shkin—*skin* right now." Tanya giggled. "I guess I'm a little drunk, Sweetie."

She let her hand wander between her legs as she drank from the bottle. She slowly stroked her clit, slicking her fingers with her juices.

Heat rushed through Tanya's body. Her nipples hardened and her breathing quickened. She took one more drink, then let the bottle fall onto the bed, soaking the sheets with the remaining liquid.

Tanya gently stroked her clit, moving her hips as she imagined Greg on top of her. She put her fingers in her pussy, but cried out in frustration. She wanted to be filled with Greg's hardness. Desperately she grabbed the Scotch bottle and inserted the neck inside her.

The bottle filled her physically, but it wasn't enough. Tanya still craved Greg. She needed to feel him warm against her skin. She took the bottle out and threw it against the wall, barely hearing it shatter.

She looked at the brass urn on the nightstand.

"You don't belong in that cold jar." She leaned over to pick up the urn. She held it tightly to her chest, smiling through her tears. "You belong with me." Tanya opened the urn and upended it, sprinkling Greg's ashes over her body. She dropped the urn off the side of the bed, then began rubbing the ashes over her sticky skin. Patches of gray ash decorated her breasts and stomach.

The ashes felt coarse against her smooth skin. She imagined Greg's face, rough with stubble, scratching her as he kissed the length of her body.

"I want you inside me," she whispered. She rubbed ashes onto her clit, the scooped some onto her fingers. Slowly Tanya let her fingers glide into her wet pussy. She ignored the coarse texture of the ashes and pretended she was feeling the bumps and ridges of Greg's hard cock.

"God, that feels good, Greg. You're such a good lover." Her hips moved quickly as she fucked her fingers. She closed her eyes and imagined him leaning over her, his hard cock thrusting in and out.

Tanya clenched the sheets with her other hand, not realizing she had bumped the ashtray, knocking her smoldering cigarette onto the bed. She didn't notice the growing heat next to her writhing body. Her orgasm was quickly approaching. She fucked her fingers faster and harder, picturing Greg naked and healthy on top of her.

Suddenly she arched her back and cried out as her orgasm ripped through her. She withdrew her fingers and sucked on them. She used to do that to Greg, suck his cock right after she came. But the taste of ashes mingled with her pussy juices jolted Tanya out of her fantasy.

She sobbed and covered her face with her hands, shaking her head from side to side.

"I can't live like this, I can't."

Abruptly she gasped in pain and opened her eyes.

"Oh my God!" The sheets had caught fire. The flames licked her breasts.

Yet she didn't try to escape. She knew she should get up and run for the extinguisher; instead, she welcomed the pain. Her skin began to blister. She closed her eyes to listen to the crackle of the fire, sure she had heard a voice whispering to her. The flames kissed her stomach and legs.

This is where I'll find Greg. This is where I need to be.

She reached between her legs once more to stroke herself. With a deep breath, Tanya embraced the fire. Embraced Greg.

As the flame licked and devoured Tanya's flesh, she felt herself approaching another orgasm. Her skin blackened and peeled, yet she kept fingering her clit. She made love to the flames, and screamed in pain and ecstasy when her orgasm tore through her body.

"I love you," a voice whispered—and before she lost consciousness, Tanya couldn't be sure it was her own.

Once I got back into writing, I submitted to more anthologies. There weren't as many print magazines as before; digital 'zines were easier to publish. But calls for submissions to print anthologies hadn't diminished. 2012 Daily Flash (366 Days of Flash Fiction) published this story.

WATCH YOUR STEP

When the holes first appeared, it wasn't so bad. They were mostly just divots, really. Sure they caused a few broken ankles and bruised egos when people got a foot caught in one, but they were basically harmless. Weird, of course; nobody could figure out why holes suddenly opened all over the city, but if you watched your step, you would be OK. And the holes closed up soon after they appeared.

I twisted my ankle in one while playing Frisbee with my friends in Central Park, but I was more embarrassed than hurt.

I doubt I'll ever live it down; they razzed me all night at the bar.

I swore that the hole wasn't there when I stepped back; it just randomly opened up. But when we looked a few minutes later, it was gone.

That scared me.

After a while, people adjusted. We New Yorkers always do. Until the holes got bigger, deeper. I saw one hole open up and swallow a man to his chest. Thankfully he was pulled out before it closed.

Then pets started disappearing. Holes even opened up in the streets and on the sidewalks. Street vendors lost their livelihoods. Traffic was a mess all the time; it looked like the city was overrun with potholes and sinkholes.

People quit driving. At least when you walked, you could carefully navigate the holes.

Until one opened up right beneath you.

At first, the holes were only in New York City. Or so we thought.

Reports started coming in from all over the place—little nothing towns, big cities; nowhere was safe. Even the president had to be pulled out of one by the Secret Service; she fell while playing tennis with her daughter.

But now I think we're all in big trouble. The holes are closing up faster.

My friends and I were out in the park a few days ago, playing Frisbee again. My friend Tim was swallowed into a hole while running—this time it closed up too fast. Only his head and one arm could be seen.

Tim screamed for us to dig him out; we called 9-1-1, but he died before they got there. The paramedics said pressure crushed him.

And the holes are getting bigger and bigger. I thought I'd be safe in my apartment, but the other night I was woken up by a God-awful rumbling sound. When I got up, I realized the building across the street was gone. Just ... gone.

And I imagine all those people who were sleeping when it happened are gone as well.

Is it safer to be on water? I don't know. When I took the ferry to work, I noticed there were fewer boats in the harbor yesterday. It could be a coincidence.

But I don't really want to know.

I think it's the end for us, I really do.

Today I watched the Statue of Liberty disappear.

I was so excited when Kasey Lansdale accepted my story to her anthology, Fresh Blood, Old Bones 2012. The "old bones" included seasoned writers such as Joe Lansdale and Nancy Collins. The "fresh blood" included up-and-comers such as Monica O'Rourke and John Paul Allen.

SACRIFICIAL LAMBS

"Damn it, Evan! Get back here right now!" Sheila put her hands on her hips and glared at her seven-year-old son.

"You can't make me!" The little redhead stood at the other end of the playground, almost beautiful in his defiance.

Sheila opened her mouth to yell at her son again when Danny, her three-year-old, ran up and kicked her leg. He giggled and ran off to join his brother, his short blond hair glistening in the sun.

Sheila sank down in the gravel and started to cry. Her boys were out of control and she had no idea what to do about it. She wiped her eyes and wearily got to her feet. "We're going home—*now!*" she shouted. She hoped they were finally done giving her a hard time for a while.

The kids stuck their tongues out at her and climbed the monkey bars. Sheila stomped toward them; she'd pull them off the equipment by their fucking throats if she had to. She grabbed each boy by his waist and sat them down hard on the ground. "Christ almighty, it's no wonder your father left! I just wish I'd left first, then he'd be stuck with you instead of me!"

The boys stared at the ground; tears rolled slowly down Danny's face.

Shit. Sheila bent down to pick up the three-year-old, but her older son pushed her hands off his little brother.

"I wish you *would* leave! I hate you!" Evan got up and took Danny by the hand. He practically dragged Danny over to the swings.

Sheila sat on a nearby bench. She put her head in her hands and began to cry once more. "I hate my life! I fucking hate it! Why were they ever born?"

"Excuse me."

Goddamn it, just leave me alone!

Sheila glanced up to see a woman was looking at her with concern.

"I'm sorry, but I couldn't help overhearing, and I saw the rough time you're having with your sons."

"Look, lady ... I'm just having a bad day. I don't need any lectures on how to raise my kids, or threats that you're going to report me." Sheila took a pack of cigarettes from her backpack and lit one up almost belligerently.

"That's not why I approached you, trust me. I have something to give you that just might help you. Oh, and by the way, my name's Abby." She held out her perfectly manicured hand to Sheila, who shook it hesitantly.

Abby rummaged through her purse, giving Sheila a chance to look her over.

I wish I could look that good, Sheila thought. It was obvious that Abby's curly auburn hair was professionally cared for on a regular basis. Her clothes definitely weren't bought at Walmart—not to mention they were actually clean. No sticky chocolate fingerprints adorned her wrinkle-free blouse.

Sheila ran a hand through her stringy brown hair, which was noticeably streaked with gray. She hadn't bought new clothes in years, not even at Walmart. What little money she could scrape together was resentfully spent on her sons' needs.

"Ah! Here we are." Abby smiled and handed Sheila a slip of paper. It was a business card, light blue with gold lettering.

H*O*M*E*S

Helping Oppressed Mothers Experience Salvation

Great. A religious freak. "Well, thank you for the card. But I don't think a church group is something I'm looking for." Sheila looked around for her boys so she could make a quick exit.

Abby put her hand on Sheila's arm. "You misunderstand. We have no religious affiliations. This is a special group; you won't find us in the yellow pages. Our members are by invitation only. You need help; we can help you. Look, we're having a meeting tonight at my house." Abby fumbled around in her purse once more and brought out a pen. She took the card from Sheila and scribbled an address on the back. "Please come. You can bring the boys if you can't get a sitter. We meet at 8:00."

Abby stood up and smiled at Sheila. "I hope I see you tonight." She walked away, her heels clicking through the gravel.

Sheila watched her leave and then looked at the card. *Wouldn't hurt to check it out. Maybe I'll even make a friend.* "Let's go *now*, boys, or I'm leaving without you!" She stalked off in the direction of their apartment, not bothering to see whether her sons were following. It didn't matter to her either way.

The boys sat at the kitchen table eating their bowls of macaroni and cheese. They were already in their pajamas. Sheila sat with them, sipping a glass of Scotch and staring morosely at the peeling wallpaper. Food-caked dishes were piled high in the sink; a few cockroaches skittered around them. *Christ, this place is a shithole.*

"You stupid-head!" Danny's shrill voice startled Sheila out of her thoughts. She looked over to see them sporting yellowish-orange noodles in their hair. Anger flared up in her and she flung her glass against the wall. The Scotch left an amber stain on the dirty yellow wallpaper.

The boys started giggling. Sheila quickly got up out of her chair, knocking it over. She leaned over the table and slapped her sons in quick succession, leaving an angry red handprint on each child's cheek. They sat in stunned silence for a few seconds, identical expressions of shock and betrayal plain on their faces.

"You little brats go to your room right now! Don't even think of getting out of those beds!" Sheila heard herself screaming like a shrew, and she cringed inside. She had become a bitch just like her mother, but she was powerless to stop it. Her sons ran crying to their room. The bedroom door slammed, causing Sheila to jump.

I gotta get out of here before I go completely insane. She suddenly remembered her encounter with the lady—*Abby, that was her name*—in the park that afternoon. She grabbed her backpack off the kitchen counter and looked through it until she found the card. *Abby said 8:00.* Sheila glanced up at the clock. She had an hour to get there.

She had no intention of taking the boys. She would have to get them cleaned up and dressed, and she didn't have the time. She opened the cabinet above the refrigerator and took out the bottle of cough syrup. She'd give the boys just enough to make sure they'd stay asleep while she was gone. She only resorted to this little trick once in a while, usually when she felt the need to get out for a few drinks. She felt a slight twinge of guilt but not enough to make her reconsider. She made her way to the boys' room, armed with the medicine and a new sense of purpose.

"Nice place, lady." The cab driver's words were an understatement. Abby's house (*Mansion*, Sheila thought, *it's a fucking mansion*) was an impressive sight to someone who had grown up in a trailer park. An iron fence surrounded the brick structure. The white pillars at the front of the house shined brightly in the moonlight. Sheila would've bet her life that she'd find a pool somewhere on the property.

"You gettin' out or what? I gotta make a livin', you know."

Sheila handed the driver some bills she had taken from Evan's piggy bank and got out of the car. The driver sped off, leaving her standing in front of the iron gate. She noticed a speaker box and timidly pushed the button.

"Yes?" A man's voice boomed through the speaker, startling Sheila.

"Um, hello? I was invited here tonight by Abby?" Sheila's voice rose questioningly, afraid she had come to the wrong house.

"Of course. You may enter." The gates slowly swung open.

Sheila walked through, wondering what lay ahead for her in that house.

Sheila followed the man dressed formally in black through the halls of the house. She assumed he was the man who had buzzed her in. She had to walk quickly to keep up with his stride. She caught only glimpses of rooms they passed. What she saw made her wish she could explore those rooms at her leisure.

One room boasted shelves from floor to ceiling filled with books. A fireplace blazed invitingly next to an overstuffed wing chair. Another room contained countless CDs and DVDs encased in glass cabinets. Sheila assumed she'd find a TV and stereo system somewhere in the room.

They finally came to a stop in front of a closed door. The man rapped twice and then opened the door.

"A Miss Sheila is here for the meeting, Mrs. Denton." He stood aside and let Sheila enter the room.

"Thank you, Portman."

Portman bowed and walked back down the hall.

Abby moved toward Sheila with her hands outstretched. "I was hoping you would make it," she said. Abby took Sheila's hands in her own. "I really think we can help you. Would you like something to drink? Coffee, perhaps?"

Sheila withdrew her hands from Abby's and nervously glanced around the room. "Could I have a Scotch, please?"

"Certainly." Abby made her way to the small bar across the room.

Several other women stood around the room, talking quietly amongst themselves. They were as well-dressed and confident as Abby, but a couple looked as defeated as Sheila. She wondered just what kind of salvation these women had to offer.

"Okay, ladies, let's sit down and get started." Abby gestured to the couch and chairs.

Sheila chose a chair that was set a little apart from the rest of the group. For the first time she noticed a couple of pictures on the marble coffee table. She leaned forward to get a closer look.

Once she recognized the faces in the frames, her curiosity was piqued further.

Sheila had seen those faces many times before. Diane Downs and Susan Smith were two of the most famous mothers in the country. And while Sheila had been as horrified as everyone else when these mothers cold-bloodedly murdered their own children, a part of her could relate to the desperation behind their actions.

"We have three new members with us today."

Sheila was brought back to the present at the sound of Abby's voice.

"Linda, Sheila, and Jackie—welcome to our group. We're glad you took the first step toward improving your lives."

"So, just how are you supposed to help us?" A slightly overweight black woman sat back on the couch with her arms folded across her chest. "You going to give us a million dollars or something? 'Cause that's the only thing that will improve *my* life."

Abby smiled indulgently at the woman. "No, Jackie. We provide you with something much more valuable. Allow me to explain.

"I was once just like the three of you. Desperate, hopeless, angry. My life was a complete waste. And all because I'd made the mistake of becoming a mother." The other well-dressed women nodded and murmured in agreement.

"My daughter took up every minute of my day. Always demanding something from me, never listening, constantly misbehaving. It got to the point where I could barely stand to be around her for any length of time. The endless stress was taking a toll on my marriage. My husband and I were drifting apart, fighting all the time. We were both completely miserable. It was a nightmarish time. But I didn't know how to wake up and take my life back. Then one day something happened that changed everything."

Sheila leaned forward, mesmerized by Abby's story. Abby noticed and smiled at her.

"Jenna and I were at the mall. As usual she needed clothes, shoes, whatever. Only four years old, but I was always shelling out money for one need or another. We could afford it, but it still irritated me. And as usual, she was acting up the entire time. She was pissing me off left and right. Finally I decided we needed to take a break, so we went over to the food court for a snack.

"I sat her down at a table and went to get us a pretzel and soda. When I got back a few minutes later, she was gone. I was angry at first because I had told her not to move. I called for her and looked around, but I couldn't see her. Finally a man at a nearby table told me a man had left with Jenna; he had just assumed the man was Jenna's father. I called the police, called my husband. Mall security locked all the exits, but the man who had taken Jenna was long gone.

"They found her body just hours later."

The three new members gasped. "I'm so sorry, Abby," Linda said. The teen mom with blonde hair was badly in need of a touch-up. She wiped at her eyes.

Sheila never took her eyes off of Abby. She was enthralled by the woman's story.

Abby shook her head slightly at Linda's expression of sympathy. "We were sad at first, of course. And I felt terrible that she had died such a horrible death all alone. But after a few months we realized our lives had changed. With Jenna gone, our lives became calm. There was no more screaming, no more stress. James and I started getting along for the first time in years, actually falling in love again. We agreed we'd never have any more children."

"God, you sound pretty heartless," Jackie said. "Don't you miss your baby at all?"

"Honestly? Not really. Once in a while I'll think about her. But she's much better off now. The whole experience showed me that I'm just not cut out to be a mother. Not every woman is. Some women know this—but others don't discover it until it's too late."

Sheila spoke for the first time since Abby began telling her story. "So what does all this have to do with us? What kind of 'help' are you actually providing? And why do you have pictures of Diane Downs and Susan Smith? What have they got to do with this?"

"Downs and Smith are examples of how not to deal with your problems. They discovered they weren't meant for motherhood but tried to take care of the situation themselves. Now they're in jail, probably for life. They were desperate—and stupid. We're here to make sure you're not."

"I still don't understand, Abby. How are you planning to help us?" Sheila was tingling with anticipation; she had the feeling this woman *could* help her in some way. She felt almost hopeful, an unfamiliar emotion of late.

Abby sank down in a chair facing the group. "After Jenna was taken and everything finally settled down, it occurred to me that my problem had been solved in an extremely tidy manner. Unlike Downs and Smith, someone else really had taken my daughter. I wasn't under any suspicion, I had the sympathy of the community, and I got my life back—it was perfect."

Jackie, the black woman, jumped up from her seat. "Wait a minute—are you telling me we should kill our kids? Are you fuckin' kidding me? You are one sick bitch, lady!"

"No, of course not." Abby motioned the woman to sit back down.

Jackie reluctantly complied, a look of suspicion on her face.

"Haven't you been listening? Women who kill their kids are usually caught. They're sent to prison for life and reviled by the public. You can't get a fresh start that way. But you can start a new life if someone else takes care of the problem for you." She gazed intently at the new members. "We provide that someone else."

"Oh my God! What a horrible thing to suggest!" Linda put her hands over her face and vigorously shook her head.

"What kind of people do you think we are?" Jackie stared at Abby with a look of disgust on her face. "I was right—you *are* a sick bitch. Let's get out of here." She looked at Linda and Sheila and motioned to them to follow her.

Linda got up and grabbed her purse.

Sheila didn't move. The other two looked at her in disbelief.

"You're just as fucked up as she is." Jackie glanced around at the group. "I'm sure the police will be real interested in this little 'club.'" She and Linda stormed out of the room.

Abby casually made her way across the room and picked up a phone sitting on top of the bar. She punched in a number and waited for an answer.

"Portman? Yes, two of our guests are leaving." Abby paused, listening. "No, they won't be returning, they made their intentions quite clear. Please proceed as usual for this situation. Thank you." She hung up the phone and turned to the group.

"So what's going to happen to them?" Sheila asked.

Abby smiled at her. "Don't worry about them. Let's start helping you get your life back."

Abby and Sheila sat on the couch together drinking coffee. The other women had left a little while before.

"Is there a man in your life, Sheila?"

Sheila shook her head and put her cup and saucer on the table. "My husband left me about a year ago. I have no idea where he is. No man has looked my way since. Not that there's any reason to look at me anyway."

"Don't put yourself down, Sheila." Abby smiled and patted Sheila's knee. "You'll be beautiful again. I promise. And it actually makes things easier if you don't have a man. Downs and Smith killed their children because their boyfriends didn't like kids. That was their biggest downfall. Never do anything drastic for a man. They're just not worth it."

Sheila smiled wanly. "You got that right."

Abby clapped her hands together. "Okay! Let's get this planned out for you. I'm sure you'd like to start your new life as soon as possible."

Sheila lay in bed, staring at the ceiling. Sleep would not come to her this night. She knew what she had agreed to was wrong, probably even evil, but she couldn't help feeling excited. In just a few short weeks, she'd be free. She could live again, not just exist.

"It'll happen when you least expect it," Abby had said. "That way, your shock is genuine and you won't be under suspicion. We use many different methods. I won't tell you how it's going to go down. Go home and try to forget about this evening. Oh, and just so you know—your children won't suffer. It will all be over quickly."

The first few days after the meeting were difficult for Sheila. Whenever she would venture out with the kids, she'd glance about nervously, wondering if today was the day. But eventually Sheila started to relax. There was light at the end of the tunnel for her, and that helped get her through the days. She felt her depression lifting, and she cut down on her drinking. For the first time in a long time, she was almost happy.

As if inspired by the changes in their mother, the boys fought less and played together more. Both were nicer to Sheila, even showing her genuine affection on occasion. To reward them for their recent good behavior, Sheila promised them a trip to the zoo the following day.

They couldn't have asked for more delightful weather; it was one of those rare midsummer days when the humidity is low and the sun is pleasantly warm. Sheila and the boys walked hand in hand, stopping to look at their favorite animals. Danny giggled uncontrollably at the monkeys' silly antics. Evan clapped his hands excitedly as he watched the lion cubs play in the grass.

"How about some ice cream, guys?" Sheila offered. "I'll bet they've got chocolate!"

"Yeah!"

"Oh, boy!"

Sheila settled them at a table in the Snack Shack and then walked to the counter to order the treats. She heard the screams as she handed her money to the clerk.

Fear stabbed at Sheila's heart when she realized what was happening. She whipped around, knocking the ice cream off the counter. Two men were dragging her sons out the door. Terror distorted the boys' features and tears streamed down their cheeks.

"No!" Sheila screamed. "Not my babies! I'm sorry! Don't do this, I don't want this to happen!"

She ran after them, pushing through the milling crowd, pleading for her children's lives. She saw the men whisk her children into a waiting car. Evan and Danny's faces were pressed against the rear window; their mouths wide with silent screams. Sheila fell to her knees with her head in her hands. Several people rushed to her side, while others called 9-1-1 on their cell phones.

Sheila desperately pushed the button on the gate outside Abby's house.

"Yes? May I help you?" Sheila recognized the man's voice from the last time she had been there.

"I need to see Abby—please let me in!" She was afraid the man wouldn't allow her entrance.

"Miss Abby's been expecting you, Miss Sheila. Please proceed."

Abby sat calmly on the couch, listening to Sheila beg for her sons' return.

"I don't want to go through with this! I love them. They're my babies, for Christ's sake! Please give them back to me—I'll never tell about this, I swear!" Sheila's face was streaked with the tears she'd been crying all afternoon. She had cooperated with the police but knew they'd never find her boys. As soon as she left the police station, she'd grabbed a taxi to Abby's.

"I'm sorry, Sheila." Abby's voice was gentle. "It's already been done."

Sheila covered her face with her hands and shook her head. "What have I done? My poor little boys. I can never forgive myself."

Abby put her arm around Sheila. "I know it's hard. All the women feel that way at first. You'll feel sad and guilty for a while. But eventually you're going to start feeling a little better. And one day you'll realize that you're much happier than you ever thought you could be."

"No. I don't know how I'm going to live with myself. There's no way I'll ever be happy again."

Abby smiled knowingly. "We've all said that after losing our children. But I promise you, things will be very different down the road. And you can take comfort in the fact that your children didn't suffer."

Sheila sobbed as her heart shattered into pieces. She put her head on Abby's shoulder and wondered if she'd be able to get through the pain.

I'm not much for writing about "real" monsters, but when I saw a call for Bigfoot stories, I couldn't resist. This was published in Bigfoot Terror Tales Volume 2: More Scary Stories of Sasquatch Horror, edited by Eric S. Brown and A. P. Fuchs in 2013.

MATERNAL INSTINCT

A ny day now. It will come any day now.

The midwife's prediction had nearly become a prayer to Jessica by now. She couldn't wait to get home and tell Dean. Their first baby, a son, could be held as soon as tomorrow. The nursery was ready; *she* was ready. After enduring three miscarriages and seemingly endless infertility treatments, she was understandably anxious.

The light turned red.

Jessica took the opportunity to caress her huge belly, barely fitting behind the Saturn's steering wheel. As if acknowledging his mother's touch, the baby pushed against the walls of her uterus; his tiny foot was clearly visible through the flimsy fabric of her blouse. A maternal smile lit the expectant mother's face.

An impatient honk jolted her out of reverie; she glanced up at the green light, seeing thick white flakes tumble and dance in the sky. They melted on the hood of her car.

Home was still about an hour away.

Would the roads get too slick? she wondered. The snow fell harder the closer she got to home. She and Dean had purchased the converted barn and its surrounding acres during the summer and hadn't really thought about the isolation that winter could bring.

The house had captivated them immediately, capturing their hearts during the first tour of it. It had a wrap-around porch, a pot-bellied stove in the kitchen, plenty of bedroom space, storage—all the things she wanted in a house. Whenever she stepped through the kitchen door, it felt like entering a time warp to a simpler life.

She thought it was the perfect place to raise a family.

The wipers whipped across the windshield, but were no match for the snow. Even with her high beams on, Jessica could only see a couple of feet ahead. Already, a few inches had fallen and she was forced to drive at a snail's pace or fear running off the sides of the road, bordered by pine trees. They bent under the snow's heavy weight.

It felt like driving through a dimly lit tunnel.

Icy fingers of claustrophobia danced up her spine, making her shiver. The baby squirmed constantly, as if sensing his mother's anxiety.

Please just let me get home safely, Jessica thought. *I'm scared.*

She stepped on the gas just a little bit harder. This leg of the trip always made her a nervous wreck because the road became one lane, surrounded by woods. Only the locals traveled it, and not by choice. She wished Dean had gone with her to the doctor so she wouldn't be driving this road alone.

A black shape darted from the trees and into the Saturn's path. She yelled, cranking the wheel to the right and fishtailing toward the side of the road. The front tires rolled heavily over something that felt like a speed bump.

Finally, the car's front end landed in a ditch and the motor cut out. Jessica broke into tears, protectively checking her belly. "Are you okay, little one?" she asked. "Are you okay?"

The baby gently kicked, almost reassuringly.

Jessica cried harder, simply relieved. She took deep breaths and tried to focus before attempting to start the car back up. It weakly coughed, sputtered and died.

Don't panic, she told herself. *This is why Dean bought you a cell phone.*

She reached for the tattered backpack on the passenger seat and rummaged around inside. Panic rose when she couldn't feel her phone.

Relax. Take your time.

She sifted through the junk, taking out her wallet, the most recent paperback by Nicholson and a pack of tissues. "Gah, where the hell is the stupid thing?"

Frantic, she turned the backpack upside down and dumped the rest of the stuff onto the seat next to her.

No phone.

A second later and a snapshot of the small red phone popped up still hooked to the charger on the kitchen counter, clear as day in her mind's eye. In her rush to make her appointment she must have completely forgotten it. With a cry of frustration, she swept her junk onto the floor.

Jessica wept again, laying her head on the steering wheel. *This is bad,* she thought. *I'm really in trouble.*

She leaned back against the seat and closed her eyes, trying to catch her breath and assess the situation.

Okay. She made a fist and stuck out a finger for each item she mentally counted off. *Car's stuck, won't start. No cell phone. Snow too thick to walk through, even if I wasn't nine months pregnant. On top of everything else, I could go into labor at any time.*

Crap.

Jessica's eyes flew open; panic fluttered in her chest again, making it hard to breathe.

Come on, now, Dean knows I'm due home soon. If I'm late, he'll worry. He'll probably even come after me if he can't reach me on the cell. Hopefully he'll see it sitting on the counter. Just wait a little while. His truck will come. Slightly comforted by this thought, she closed her eyes again and started to relax. Fatigued from the pregnancy, it was easy to drift off to sleep.

Nightmares could wait.

A scraping sound, like fingernails down a chalkboard, startled Jessica awake. *What was that?*

Darkness had fallen and the blanket of snow had taken on a bluish tinge, still steadily coming down. *Must've been dreaming.*

Jessica looked at her watch. 5:15.

Only about an hour had passed. She felt cold, hungry and she desperately had to pee. The baby had settled in his favorite spot, right on her bladder.

Dean should be coming any minute, she thought. *I know he will. He has to.*

Resigned to peeing on the side of the road, Jessica grabbed the door handle and started to pull.

The scratching sound returned.

Now that she was awake, she realized it was coming from the other side of the door she'd almost opened.

Maybe it's that poor animal I must've run over. I wonder if it's hurt?

Her maternal instincts kicked in; she gently opened the door to check the injured creature. At first glance, the creature looked like a bear cub. Its brown-black fur was matted and bloody. But what should've been its front legs looked like arms, and what should've been paws looked like misshapen, broken hands.

The creature's breathing was labored and she saw two rows of razor-sharp teeth in its mouth, below the blood oozing from its snout. Malevolent red eyes shot open, gazing into her own blue ones. It growled a deep, inhuman sound, not unlike a bear. She slammed the car door shut, muffling her screams of terror.

Please, Dean. Come find me.

The creature switched to odd mewling sounds mixed with human crying. Her heart went out to the injured creature. It didn't move.

After wrestling with her thoughts for a few minutes, she opened the door again. She tossed her coat from the back seat onto the now-unconscious animal. Hesitantly, she reached down and touched the fur on its exposed leg.

Instead of coarse hairs, the fur was soft and silky, like the flaxen hair of children. Stroking the animal's head, she felt its body shake as it forced its breathing. If she had her cell, she could call Animal Control. She didn't want the creature to die.

Reluctantly, but shivering from the cold, she shut her door and settled in to wait for her husband and the phone he would inevitably bring.

*H*ours later, Jessica saw lights coming towards her. "Dean! Oh, thank God!" It seemed to take forever, but the Chevy finally stopped a few feet away from her. Jessica rolled down her window as Dean got out of the truck.

"Oh, Dean, I've been so scared," she said, starting to cry.

"Are you okay, honey? I've been worried sick about you! I saw the cell phone on the counter and when you didn't get home on time, I panicked. The doctor's office said you left hours ago. I'm so sorry, but I'm glad I found you." As he walked to the car, he stopped short. "What the hell is *that?*"

"I don't know what it is, but it's badly hurt and it growled at me. I ran over something and I'm pretty sure ... oh, do you think I killed it?"

"I don't know. It looks like a bear, maybe a cub?" He knelt down to look the creature over.

"It's definitely not a bear. The fur feels like, I don't know, human hair, maybe. Like a baby's. It's really weird."

Dean moved her coat out of the way and put his hand on the creature's side. "It doesn't feel like it's breathing. I think it died."

Jessica's heart ached, like she had run over a neighbor's pet. "Poor thing. Dean, can we just go home now?"

"Yeah, okay. I'll call the sheriff when we get back." He stood up and reached for the door handle.

An agonized howl came from the trees, making their blood run cold.

"What was that?" Dean asked. He turned around. Jessica, too.

An obviously female creature lurched out from the trees. Her breasts hung low and heavy, dripping milky fluid.

She ran toward them, her belly as round and full as Jessica's. Black-brown fur covered her body as well.

The beast saw Dean standing over her child on the road. It screamed, saliva splattering Dean's face as the beast batted him aside like a mere doll. He flew through the air and landed face down in the snow, rolling onto his back. He moaned, unmoving.

The mother crouched down and gathered up her dead child. Gently, she rocked its body, nuzzling her cheek against the tiny face. Her sad, soft keening broke through the couple's stunned silence.

Dean pulled himself to his knees, slowly. Somehow, he managed to stand, but Jessica was worried the creature would take notice and go after him. The sound of his boots crunching through the snow seemed almost deafening. He inched his way to Jessica and the Saturn.

Before she could warn him, the beast's head whipped around. The creature put her child down on the snow with slow and gentle hands, then turned back to him. Screaming as she ran, she clawed his face, slicing the flesh to ribbons.

"Dean!" Jessica screamed. "No, please don't hurt him!" Her hands flew to her mouth; her son thrashed and kicked inside.

The mother-beast yanked Dean up by his throat. He helplessly kicked his legs in the air. He grabbed the beast's wrist in a futile effort to free himself. Her enraged eyes locked with his.

Jessica screamed. "Put him down! Oh, no. Dean!"

The creature threw Dean onto the road and fell upon him. She opened her mouth wide; it was filled with two rows of sharp teeth. She leaned down and in one swift bite tore out his throat completely.

Jessica let go of the urine she'd been holding in for so long and protectively clutched her stomach. Her teeth chattered and her breath hitched in horrified gasps. The mother-creature raised her head and sniffed at the air, Dean's blood dripping from her mouth.

She lumbered over to Jessica's car. Frantically, Jessica rolled up the window and locked the doors.

I'm sorry. I'm sorry, she thought, wishing she could communicate with it, *but please go away. Please, God, make her go away.*

Jessica curled up in her seat as best she could. The pungent smell of ammonia assaulted her senses, but she didn't dare open the window, even just a crack to let out the stench. Her skirt and panties were soaked, but she couldn't do anything about it.

She lowered her forehead to her drawn-up knees and softly sobbed. Everything sounded eerily quiet, but she was too afraid to look. If the thing that murdered her husband was still out there, she knew it would kill her, too. She needed to get to Dean's truck to escape, but with the monster somewhere nearby, the truck might as well have been a million miles away. She couldn't run, not in her condition. She had to check for the beast, though. She and her baby would die if she didn't make it to the truck.

Cautiously, she rolled down her window and looked around. She couldn't see anything, but she heard a low growl somewhere close by. She quickly rolled up the window. Exhausted and emotionally drained, she cried herself to sleep.

Gruesome flashes of her husband's death wove together with images of the big beast ripping her unborn son from her womb.

She awoke with a start; her back ached and her body shivered. Her coat was still outside the car door. Jessica looked around for the beast, but saw nothing. The snow had stopped and the moon peeked out from behind dark clouds. Snow sparkled and glistened in the dim moonlight. It would've been a beautiful scene if not for Dean's bloody, lifeless body sprawled on the road. She held her hands over her mouth, heaving deep, silent sobs. She averted her eyes; she couldn't think about her husband yet. Not out here. Not like this.

She opened her door a few inches, cringing as the hinges squeaked, despite her careful efforts to go slowly. The coat was barely within reach, lying beside the dead monster's baby. Why had the mother-creature left her dead child behind? She stretched her arm toward the coat, but couldn't quite get it. She grabbed the steering wheel with her right hand and leaned a little further, reaching for the coat with her left. She pulled the coat into the car when a furry black hand shot up from behind the door and yanked her wrist.

She screamed and desperately kicked at the creature's hand. As she struggled to free herself, she lost her grip on the steering wheel and accidently honked the horn. The beast roared at the noise, holding its ears and letting go of Jessica's wrist.

Breathing hard and sobbing, Jessica dropped the coat and scrambled back into the car. The door slammed hard enough to rattle the windows. A contraction tore through her body and she screamed again, this time in pain. It squeezed her insides, making her feel as if she was in a vise. Just when she thought she might pass out from the pain, it subsided.

She leaned back in the seat, trying to catch her breath and calm down.

Then her water broke.

"No! No, I can't!" she said. The water gushed from her body and streamed down her legs. Another contraction wracked her body and she moaned in terror and agony.

The mother-creature stood up immediately and peered into the car window with bloodshot eyes. The beast's eyes darkened in recognition of what was happening to her. She pounded on the window, baring her sharp teeth.

"Go away!" Jessica yelled. "Leave me alone. You killed my husband, now leave me alone!" Another contraction tore through her body, causing her belly to heave and ripple.

The mother-creature pointed at Jessica's stomach and howled.

"This is my baby!" Jessica screamed. "Mine. Now go away!" She tightly closed her eyes, retreating into the age-old childhood rule that said if you close your eyes, the monster couldn't see you.

The creature backed away from the window.

Jessica leaned back in the seat, keeping her eyes squeezed shut. *Please let labor take a long time,* she begged God or whomever would listen. *Maybe someone will come by. Maybe ... maybe ...*

She caressed her stomach, trying to will the baby to stay inside. The contractions continued every few minutes, but not as intensely as before. That was a good sign, she hoped.

She opened her eyes, praying the creature would be gone. She didn't see it. *Good. Maybe she went back into the woods,* she thought. She closed her eyes and took deep breaths, trying to control her fear. Pain became as overwhelming as her emotions.

Jessica was able to calm down a little and opened her eyes. But then she saw Dean's body, partly covered in snow, and tears filled her eyes. It was still dark and now the moon brightly shone overhead. Her lips were dry and cracked from dehydration. She wished for a bottle of water.

Suddenly, she had an uncontrollable urge to bear down. No. I can't have to push already. The doctor said it would take hours, maybe days of labor for a first baby. But she had no choice. This baby was coming.

Sobbing, she took off her wet skirt and panties and threw them in the back seat. She turned around and leaned up against the door, making sure it was locked. Then she felt down between her legs.

Oh no …

She could feel her son's head beginning to crown. The baby would be delivered alone, with her husband's bloody body right outside her window.

Why me? How did this happen? The tears gushed anew.

A contraction hit her hard and instinctively she bore down and pushed, closing her eyes, screaming. She felt the baby's head tearing its way out. She leaned back again, waiting for the next contraction. She saw the beast staring at her from the passenger-side window. The creature pointed at Jessica's spread legs.

Jessica screamed again, more in fear than pain. She pushed once more, feeling the baby slip out of her. The mother-creature jumped up and down in excitement and beat on the window.

Jessica grabbed the baby and tightly held him to her chest. Another contraction tore through Jessica, this time expelling the placenta. The beast roared and hit the window with all her might. A crack zigzagged down the glass and the Saturn shook.

"No, stop! Please!" Jessica begged.

But Jessica's cries of terror only excited the mother-creature more. She pushed on the car, rocking it violently back and forth, almost tipping it over onto its side. Jessica's head slammed against the window, but she didn't let go of her son, who was now crying.

The beast punched the cracked window, shattering it. Her hairy hand reached for the baby, but Jessica scooted away until her back hit the other door. She knew her only chance would be to get to Dean's truck. Quickly, quietly, while the beast was trying to get in the broken window, Jessica opened the door and slipped out. She ran as fast as she could towards the truck, but she was weak and losing blood. The beast was on her only a few seconds later. Jessica felt hot pain across her back and fell to the ground. She tried to protect her baby, but the beast roughly rolled her over and grabbed him out of her arms. Jessica desperately tried to get up and rescue her son, but fell back to the ground, too weak to stand. She held out her arms and whispered "Please." The beast leaned over Jessica and roared, then sliced Jessica's throat with one swipe of her clawed hand.

The last thing Jessica saw was the creature carrying the baby into the woods. She heard her son's cries as her life slipped away.

Some friends in the UK put together an anthology called Ill at Ease, published in 2011. In 2013, they invited me to the second volume. Ill at Ease 2: 7 New Tales of the Macabre included authors Mark West and Stephen Bacon, and it was a fun project to participate in. My story was inspired by F. Paul Wilson's "Soft," which fascinated me.

PARADISE LOST

"My wife was furious when she discovered the digital recorder in my suitcase as she was unpacking. This was supposed to be a family retreat, yet I couldn't completely leave my work behind at home. I saw no harm in composing memos and letters as ideas came to me. I'm glad I have it now—at least I can record the events of the past few days. Luckily, this 'toy,' as Cathy referred to it, stores over two hours of recording time. I only wish I had brought my cell phone, but I knew Cathy would never forgive me. It doesn't matter now, I guess. I am glad I can record the story anyway, just in case. Just in case someone survives.

"We came to the island for a much-needed vacation, my wife, son, and I. An idyllic place in the sun, accessible only by private plane. No phones, television, radios or computers in any of the cottages; these things were located in the main lobby for emergencies only. It's a place where you can pretend 'civilization' doesn't exist. And as far as I know, it doesn't anymore. I know I'll never leave here alive, but I suppose there are worse places to die.

"I haven't left this little cottage since it happened—Christ, was it only yesterday? It was the most horrible thing I have ever witnessed. Cathy and Eric had gone out to the beach early. God, I wish I had gone with them then, but I told them I had to finish the latest Newman novel. I would join them later. That was a lie, of course. I was composing a proposal that I planned to present the minute I returned to my office. I was determined to become a partner in the firm by the end of the year. I don't know how much time had passed when the screaming started from the beach; I was totally absorbed in my dictation. The screaming was a terrible cacophony of noise; a chorus of terror and agony. I imagine Hell would be filled with that ghastly sound. I leapt off the bed and ran to the door, praying Eric and Cathy were all right.

"My first thought was that I was hallucinating, because what I saw when I flung open the door can only be described as a nightmare. I had expected to maybe see a scene straight out of that shark movie from back in the 70s. It wasn't unheard of here to spot the occasional shark. But it was something worse—much worse. Everyone on the beach was melting. *Melting!* Flesh was sliding off their bodies, the bones liquefying as soon as the skin was gone. I completely freaked—I couldn't move. Which was a good thing, I guess, because everyone who emerged from their cottages into the sun started to melt as well.

"I could smell burning hair and flesh – God, it almost smelled like the luau we went to years ago. My … my mouth actually watered for a second. But this wasn't pork cooking. Tears filled my eyes, transforming the hideous scene into a shimmering blur. I swiped at my eyes with the backs of my hands and watched in horror as tiny flames danced upon the heads of the people on the beach.

"A few people instinctively beat at the flames with their hands, but only succeeded in getting their hands stuck to their heads. Some looked up at the sky, I guess to see what was causing it, and immediately their eyes burst into flames.

"Blisters bubbled and erupted on any exposed skin, then ruptured seconds later, gushing fluid that ran in rivulets down their bodies. Finally, the skin slipped off their bones, leaving blobs of flesh upon the sand. The bones dissolved as soon as they were exposed, mixing with the melted flesh, giving it a swirled appearance. The beach looked as if a pudding factory had exploded there. Waves licked at the flaming puddles, extinguishing those closest to the shore.

"Frantically I scanned the beach for my family, praying that maybe that they had gone inside the bar hut to get a drink. Then I saw them—dear God, I saw them."

Sounds of sobbing; recording stops abruptly.

Recording starts again, the voice shaky and quiet.

"Okay … Okay. I've got to do this. If it's only happened on this island, the world needs to know the story. Sweet Jesus, I hope it only happened on this island.

"My wife and son were still on the beach. I hadn't seen them at first because I thought they were someone else. You see, at first glance they looked like one obese person—but I guess Cathy had clutched Eric to her when it began because they were melting together. They had … had *fused* together as they melted. Half of Eric's face had melted into Cathy's breast—an obscene parody of their nursing days. I'm just thankful they had worn hats onto the beach, which protected their hair from catching fire. I was able to look into Cathy's eyes before her face fell off her skull. Betrayal, fear, pain—I could see all those things. It hurts me to think she may have hated me at the end for deserting her. Maybe I should've just run out to the beach and embraced her so we could all die together. But I couldn't. I shut the door. Then I closed all the blinds and went into the bathroom. I ran the shower full-force so I wouldn't hear anymore screaming.

"All of that happened in a matter of minutes—no more than two or three. But each minute was an eternity.

"I don't know how many people on the island are still alive. I hear occasional screams outside, but I don't open the door. I have enough to survive for a while; I have no intention of sharing. There's a small kitchenette with a refrigerator stocked by the resort management."

Derisive snort

"Guess now I won't have to pay eight freaking dollars for a tiny jar of macadamia nuts. Too bad there's no vodka in the damn fridge; God knows I could use a few shots. Anyway, I figured as long as I stayed inside during the day, out of the sun, I'd be OK.

"But I was terribly wrong. Because it wasn't the sun. When the sun finally set, I opened the window blinds and looked outside. Thankfully, the sand had absorbed what had been left of the dead. No trace remained of the horror that had taken place out there. As I watched, several people stepped out of their cottages onto the beach. At first I thought everything was okay and planned to join them.

"The screaming began again, though, only this time much worse. Turns out the melting hadn't been caused by the sun, but the sun *had* helped it along and had also caused the fires and blisters. The people outside were melting, but they were melting much slower than the others had. I could see flesh dripping off their fingertips, their chins. I wondered why they didn't run inside—then it came to me a few moments later. The beach was still very hot from the sun beating down on it all day, and I saw that their feet were shapeless blobs of flesh anchored into the sand. They were like candles in a sconce, and they would stay there and drip bit by bit until there was nothing left. With a shudder I closed the blinds once more. The screaming went on all night, finally stopping a few minutes after the sun rose. If I had had a gun, I would've been dead long before they were.

"So I decided the melting was caused by the heat outside. It sounds absurd, but what else could I think? I cranked the air conditioning up full-blast and took off my clothes. I didn't want to take the chance of getting hot in any way. I was freezing, but that was better than the alternative. I kept busy that day. I had brought several novels with me, and Cathy had brought her trashy women's magazines, so I read. I wasn't too hungry, but I ate anyway, just to have something to do.

"The situation got much worse tonight. I truly don't think I'll survive much longer. The cottage became quite dark as the sun went down. I wasn't ready to sleep, although I hadn't slept at all the night before, but I did want to read a bit more. Escape from the living hell.

"I switched on the bedside lamp. As soon as the light winked on, my thumb and forefinger started melting into the brass pull-chain. I screamed—Sweet Jesus, it hurt! My hand felt like it was on fire. I tried to pull my hand out from under the lampshade, but the finger and thumb were becoming intertwined with the chain. I could see my flesh starting to pool and drip onto the nightstand. With my other hand, I grabbed the wooden base of the lamp—it was still cool, thankfully—and smashed it against the wall. The lamp broke, shattering the light bulb, but I was still stuck to it. I was too scared to rip my hand away, so I just kept smashing the lamp against the wall until it was completely destroyed. The chain remained woven through my flesh, but I wasn't going to try and get it out. What was the point? If the little bit of heat emanating from a light bulb was enough to start the melting, how the hell would I survive?

"I plunged my hand into the thawing bucket of ice I'd left on the nightstand, not caring if any shards from the lamp had gotten in it. I just wanted to stop the melting. It was a horrible feeling. My hand felt as if it were a glove that was being slowly removed. It looks as if something tried to flatten it with a meat mallet. It doesn't hurt anymore, though. In fact, I can't feel it at all. My hand is already dead—it's just waiting for the rest of me to catch up. I can't imagine what it will be like when my whole body melts.

"I don't dare turn on any other light. I guess I'll just try to sleep."

Recorder clicks off, then clicks on again; sobbing is heard.

"The air conditioning is off! It's like a fucking oven in here!"

More sobbing; incoherent words.

"Nobody will survive this. It's the end of the world, I fucking know it! We need to be warm to survive. Dear God, even people in Alaska will die—or freeze to death if they don't use heaters or fire to keep warm!"

More sobbing; terrified gibbering.

"Oh, shit. It's happening! I've started to melt! I'm sticking to the bed sheets!"

Insane laughter, slowly trailing off into quiet crying.

"I can't get off this bed. I'm going to die in a puddle on this goddamn bed!

A few moments of humming and quiet singing.

"What the fuck? What is that sound? No. Oh, no. Please, God, no! The air conditioner is back on! I forgot to set the switch to continual—the damn thing will run intermittently! It will take forever to completely melt—I can already feel myself solidifying!"

Unrelenting screams, eventually dying off to quiet sobbing.
Voice is almost unrecognizable, barely above a whisper.
"Help me ..."

This story was published in 2013 by Jacob Haddon of Apokrupha in the anthology Dark Bits. It was a fun story to write; a little sad, a little creepy, which are my favorite kind of stories.

THE LYING DEAD

Don't talk to the Dead; they lie. The angry ones do, anyway. The angry Dead purposely stay on Earth to cause trouble; the others somehow got stuck here and do their best to cope. Sometimes they even help out living humans. Trying to build up Karma, I guess.

You can tell which of the Dead are angry—they have a darkness about them; it engulfs them. You cross the street to avoid them because they'll start shit for no reason. They can't touch you, but they can still fuck with your mind and spirit. They claim to know things about people. Secret things; hurtful things. They love to use that stuff to mess up your mind, your life, your soul. They *feed* on the misery they cause.

My wife died a few weeks ago of the cancer that ravaged her body for over a year. Thankfully, she passed on to whatever is next. I miss her terribly, but I'm glad she didn't stay. Now one of the Dead is following me. He's saying things about my wife that aren't true. That she was having an affair with him when they used to work together years ago. That my son is not mine; he belongs to this Dead man. I beg him to stop lying and leave me alone, but he won't.

As I look through pictures of my wife and me with our son, he whispers behind me. *Look how he resembles me, Matthew. You know he isn't your boy.*

"Leave me alone! Just shut up!" I yell. My outburst only makes the Dead man smile.

Maybe I'll go talk to my son today. Maybe I'll tell him just what a whore his mother was.

"Please leave us in peace," I sob. "Just go away. Why are you doing this?"

Because I can. Am I lying? Telling the truth? You'll never be sure. You have doubts now about her. You'll never have another peaceful moment. Now you're like the rest of us, only Living. For now.

Then he faded away. His work with me was done. And he was right—now I have doubts. That bastard took the best part of my life and shit all over it. Maggie and I were so happy together and when Michael came along, we were ecstatic. There is no way, *no way* she slept with that guy and got pregnant with Michael.

"Hi, Daddy!" My son comes into my room and climbs up on the bed with me. I give him a hug, then gaze into his beautiful face. The face that doesn't resemble mine much at all. I say a prayer.

Dear God, please let them lie. Let the Dead lie.

This story is from Barnyard Horrors, a cool anthology published by James Ward Kirk. Scarecrows have always creeped me out and fascinated me, ever since I saw the TV movie Dark Night of the Scarecrow in the early 80s.

SCARECROW NIGHT

A my hated the annual community Scarecrow Festival. It wouldn't be so bad if the scarecrows that the farmers made for the contest were cute. But no, somehow it turned into a competition to see who could make the creepiest straw man in the county. Amy hated walking by the display once the sun set. Lit only by candles, the scarecrows were staked into the barn floor in a circle, as if facing off against one another.

Since her parents didn't like leaving her alone at night, Amy was dragged back to the Johnson farm for the evening festivities that took place after dinner. The adults drank apple cider and danced and got silly, while the kids ate the candy apples and popcorn balls Mrs. Johnson always made for them.

Henry sat on the grass next to Amy. They had been friends since they could toddle around their yards, chattering to each other through the fence that separated their farms.

"I bet the scarecrows still creep you out, don't they, Amy?"

"So what if they do? That's what they're supposed to do, moron."

Henry laughed, knowing he had gotten a rise out of her. Amy had always been afraid of the scarecrows, especially at night. She even hated the one that loomed over the field in the middle of her parents' farm for the past year. Scarecrows were replaced every year, the night after the festival, when everyone took their creations home after judging.

"Let's go look at this year's scarecrows and bet on which one is going to win tonight. You have to stop being afraid *sometime*."

"No, let's just stay here. I don't care which one wins."

"Sissy! I'm going to go look. I'm hoping my dad wins this year; he could use the money. I even helped him with it this time; he finally said I was old enough."

Amy heard the pride in her friend's voice and sighed. Henry was her best friend, and she would do anything for him if it would make him happy. Even go look at big creepy dolls made out of straw and old clothes. "Okay. But just for a few minutes—I want to see what my parents made, too. Hopefully it's not as horrible as last year's."

Henry got up and reached for Amy. She took his hand and they snuck through the shadows to the barn. Kids weren't allowed to go in the scarecrow barn at night.

The barn door was locked, but Henry knew where there were a few broken boards they could squeeze through to get inside. They crawled inside on their hands and knees, then stood up and looked around. Amy gasped and grabbed Henry's arm.

Most of the candles were burned out; hardened wax dotted the hay-covered floor. The few candles still lit flickered in the darkness, the straw men's shadows danced upon the wooden walls.

"They're horrible," Amy whispered, as if afraid they would hear her.

"I think they're cool. Come on, check out the one I made with my dad. I think it's going to win."

Henry walked into the center of the scarecrow circle, stopping in front of the most horrific one. "It's this one—check it out!"

Amy joined Henry in front of the scarecrow, then backed away a little bit when she saw its face. Although its hat obscured its face, Amy saw its eyes—they seemed to glare at her from under the brim. The eyes were completely black, and Amy could tell they were not crafted from old buttons. Henry left her side to look at the other creations, and Amy peered at Henry's scarecrow to figure out what the eyes could be.

The scarecrow winked at her.

Amy screamed and jumped back. Henry went to her, and she clung to him, crying.

"What happened? What made you scream like that?"

"The scarecrow winked at me!"

Henry laughed. "Be serious. I know they're creepy, but they're not alive, for crying out loud."

"It really did! Can we get out of here? I'm scared."

"Just a few more minutes. I want to see what your parents made." He smiled at her. "You're really spooked, so you probably imagined what happened."

"Okay. But just to see what my parents came up with this year." She brushed a tear from her eye and smiled back. "I probably did imagine it."

They looked at the tags hanging from each of the thirteen scarecrows until they found her parents' names. Amy looked behind her at Henry's scarecrow, but it didn't do anything. She sighed with relief. *I'm such an idiot.*

"Found it—wow, it's amazing!" He looked at the scarecrow in awe. Although spiked into the dirt, its feet, stuffed into heavy work boots, touched the floor. Gloved hands hung to its hips. The head lolled on its side, resting on its shoulder. Empty black holes occupied the space where eyes should be, yet it seemed to be staring right at Amy. The head was smooth, not lumpy like the others that were stuffed with newspaper. A line of stitching ran across the head from front to back. The mouth was sewn shut. A trench coat covered the body.

"I don't like it. It's too scary. Scarier than the one they made last year. Now can we get out of here? If we're caught, we'll get in big trouble." She casually glanced back at Henry's scarecrow, but it still didn't move.

"Yeah, okay. I bet your parents win the money this year."

Amy heard the dejection in Henry's voice. She knew his dad needed the money. "I'm sorry, Henry. I think your dad's scarecrow is really creepy. It could still win. I mean, look at the others—they're ugly, but not really scary like yours."

"Whatever. Let's go."

Amy started for the barn door, but Henry grabbed her arm. "We have to go the way we came, or they'll know we were here."

They turned around to go through the loose boards at the back of the barn. Before they could leave the circle, every scarecrow's arms rose up, touching one another's, barring the kids from moving past them. Amy fell on her butt trying to get away.

"What do we do? What is going on?" Amy cried, too scared to move.

"I don't know. They must be mechanical or something. The grown-ups probably know we're here and are trying to scare us. Let's just crawl under their arms."

Henry got down on his hands and knees, grumbling at the adults under his breath. His plans to finally kiss Amy were spoiled for the night. He got halfway out of the circle when the trench-coated scarecrow stomped on Henry's back with its boot. There was a loud SNAP and Henry screamed. Blood shot from his mouth, spattering the hay with red.

Amy opened her mouth to scream, but nothing came out. She crab-walked away, knowing she couldn't help Henry. She could only think of escape. She looked up at the scarecrow as she scuttled back, but this time did scream when it grinned at her. Ragged teeth jutted through the burlap as the stitching ripped open. It reached out for her, but Amy was able to run under another scarecrow's arms towards the barn door.

She pulled on the door—forgetting it was locked. She beat on it with her fists. "Help! Help me!" She turned to look at the scarecrows. *They were off the stakes, walking towards her.* Amy shrieked, then ran over to the broken boards. She wriggled out, scratching herself on the sharp edges, but didn't notice. Finally free, Amy ran screaming to the adults.

But they were gone.

The lights were out and the music silent.

Amy looked back at the barn, only to see the scarecrows emerging. She turned and ran towards her house, screaming for her parents. She could see her breath in the moonlight as she ran, panting with exertion. She heard footsteps on the dirt road behind her, but didn't dare turn around. She knew they were following her.

She sprinted across her yard to her front porch, and turned the knob on the front door. It was locked as well. She knocked on the door, bruising her knuckles, yelling for her mom and dad to save her. The porch light turned on, bathing the yard in a yellow glow. The scarecrows stood in a semi-circle in front of the house, silently waiting for something.

The front door opened, and Amy threw herself into her mother's arms, sobbing, relieved to be home. She knew her dad could take care of the scarecrows.

Her mother pushed her away, none too gently.

"You and Henry shouldn't have gone into the barn. You knew it was forbidden." The woman looked down upon Amy, no warmth in her eyes.

"Yes, Amy. You could've ruined everything." Amy shook in fear at her father's stern voice. She had never heard that voice before, even when she got in trouble for skipping school that one time.

"But—what's going on? Mom? Dad? Please help me?" Amy's voice dropped to a whisper. "Henry's in the barn still; he's hurt."

"Henry has been taken care of. Now we must deal with you. All the other kids stayed away from the barn—it's too bad you couldn't."

Amy noticed they were wearing black robes. They pulled the hoods up, then stepped out onto the porch. The other adults in the community emerged from her house as well.

"The Scarecrow Festival is important to us, Amy," her mother said. "This is a prosperous community—prosperous for those who obey. Henry's father Jim didn't want to participate this year because it was his son's turn to be sacrificed. He made the scarecrow anyway, so sure we'd think he was obeying the contract after all, but we knew. We always know. And now not only has Henry been sacrificed, but his father as well."

Amy's father shook his head. "Because you are aware of our ways now, you must be sacrificed as well. I'm sorry it has to be this way, but nothing can be done for those who disobey."

He grabbed Amy by her arms and forced her down the

porch stairs. Amy screamed, struggling against his grip, but he was too strong for her.

"Daddy, please!" Amy sobbed, her mind not comprehending what was about to happen.

"I'm not your daddy, little girl. You were only a means to an end."

He tossed her at the quiet, waiting scarecrows. They fell upon her as her screams filled the night. The adults in their black robes murmured, clasping their hands and bowing their heads reverently.

When they finished feeding, the scarecrows rose in the moonlight, blood dripping from razor-sharp teeth. They shambled towards their respective farms to keep watch in the fields.

It would be another great year for the community.

Carnivals are always a great setting for a horror story. Fox Spirit Books published this story in Noir Carnival in 2013. It was also reprinted in the 2014 anthology Widow Makers: A Benefit Anthology of Dark Fiction, in which the proceeds were donated to horror writer James Newman, who had suffered an injury that year.

THINGS HAPPEN HERE AFTER DARK

Jeff and Lisa were bored, looking for something interesting and fun to do. There wasn't much going on in their small town, especially on a chilly Friday night in autumn. They weren't supposed to be out, but they had skipped school all day and didn't want to go home just yet. Jeff had thought about stealing one of the farmer's tractors for a joyride, but then something better came to mind.

"Hey, I know what we can do."

Lisa blew a few strands of blue-tinged hair out of her eyes. "What is it? It better be something good. This night's been a crapfest so far." She hated living out here in the country. She used to live in a town that had a lot more to do; then her parents divorced and her mom moved them to this stupid town she grew up in back in the 60s.

Jeff smiled, a cigarette dangling from his lip. He took it from his mouth so he could talk. "Let's go climb to the top of the Ferris wheel." Lisa folded her arms and shook her head. "I'm serious. I know the carnival is closed for the night, but it's not like there's a fence around it to keep us out. And it's only here for one more night."

"What if we're caught? My mom will kill me if I get into trouble again. I'm not even supposed to be out with you after the last time we got caught skipping school."

"Who's going to catch us? The place is pretty much deserted right now. Come on—I thought you wanted something cool to do." Jeff wasn't worried; he knew Lisa would go along with the idea. She always wanted to please him and hated it when he got mad at her. And it would be a great story to brag about to his friends at school on Monday, if he decided to go. His dad wouldn't care as long as Jeff stayed out of his booze.

"All right. What's the worst that could happen?" Lisa shrugged. "I'll just get grounded again, big deal."

"Great. Let's go." He gave Lisa a gentle pat on the butt and they ran toward the empty carnival grounds.

The moonlight cast an eerie glow over the dark carnival. The Ferris wheel loomed over the other rides, like the T-Rex skeleton in a dinosaur museum.

"I don't know about this," Lisa said. "It looks really spooky. And how are we supposed to get to the top, anyway? It's a lot higher than I remember."

"We're gonna climb up the frame. I mean, the carnival workers do it when they put it together, so it can't be that hard. Seriously—it'll be fun. Come on. I heard you were good climbing the rope in gym class; this is no different."

Lisa looked up at the ride, which seemed so much higher than it did when she was here the other night. She pictured herself slipping and falling to her death. "Oh, screw this—I'm going home." Lisa started to walk away, but Jeff pulled on her jacket.

"C'mon, Lisa, don't be lame. It'll be fun, I promise. And after we start climbing, if you still want to stop, we'll go home."

Lisa sighed. She knew she'd do it; Jeff was a Junior and she was only a Freshman. They had known each other since Lisa had moved to town a few years ago. They lived on the same block, but only recently started going out. He was so cool and sure of himself, he could go out with any girl he wanted. She was always a little nervous that he'd break up with her, so she rarely said no to him. "Okay. Might as well."

They made their way through the carnival, passing the mini rollercoaster, a few kiddie rides, and the giant slide. Hints of cotton candy and popcorn wafted through the air. A few deflating balloons gently bounced along the ground. As they walked by a large blue tent with green stripes, they heard yells and raucous laughter.

"Must be a tent for the carnival workers," Jeff whispered.

"Oh, great. What if they hear us? Will they have us arrested? I think we should just go home." Lisa didn't really care if her mother grounded her; she was usually able to sneak out anyway, but she knew she'd be in for a lot worse if the police brought her home again.

"It's fine, come *on!*" Jeff knew he sounded irritated, but he was tired of Lisa's hesitation. Sometimes she was such a baby. He thought she was a lot cooler when he had to spend detention with her. Now she looked like he had hurt her feelings. "Sorry. I didn't mean to snap, but I really want to do this, and I thought you did too."

"Okay, but I don't want to stay too long. We can make out for a little bit when we get to the top, though."

Jeff smiled and put his arm around her. Maybe she was cool after all.

"Hey, wait. Let's listen to the workers for a minute. Maybe we'll hear something interesting."

Surprised at Lisa's sudden bravery, he knelt down with her to eavesdrop.

"Get anything good tonight, Charlie?" a voice boomed from the tent, making Lisa jump.

"Only about a hundred bucks; tonight was pretty slow. Not as many people as usual for some reason."

"Probably the cold weather. I don't know why the boss insists on traveling in the fall."

"He must be a pickpocket or something," Jeff whispered. "I've heard that a lot of carnival workers are thieves."

"Really? They were nice to me a few nights ago when I came here with my sister." Lisa was young for her age and tended to see the good in most people, even though she tried to act tough.

Jeff, amused, just shook his head.

"Whatever," Lisa said. "Let's get to the Ferris wheel; I'm getting cold."

They quietly tiptoed past the tent, not wanting to attract the men's attention. As they walked through the moonlit carnival, Lisa again grew nervous. She knew she could climb at least part way up the Ferris wheel; she sometimes went rock climbing with her dad when he was in town. That wasn't what was scaring her. But unable to put a finger on her unease, she let Jeff lead her to the towering ride.

Lisa looked up at the Ferris wheel. "Oh yeah, it's definitely a lot higher than I thought," she said. "I'm pretty sure I won't make it all the way up to the top."

Jeff wasn't sure he would either, but he wasn't about to admit it to Lisa. "Come on, we'll be fine. Just don't look down." He grabbed one of the colorful metal bars that made up the ride's frame and began to ascend.

"Oh, God. I'm an idiot." Lisa took a deep breath and followed Jeff up the ride.

About halfway up Jeff admitted to himself he couldn't make it to the top. His hands were getting sweaty, making him nervous about slipping. "How about we stop here and get in this car?" He gestured at the car closest to them. "I don't want to make you climb anymore," Jeff said to save face.

Lisa sighed with relief. "Sounds good to me. It's still an adventure, right?"

"Right." Jeff swung his legs into the car and then gingerly climbed in. He helped Lisa in once he was secure. The car rocked back and forth a bit but stopped once they were both seated.

Although they weren't all the way at the top, they could see the whole carnival in the bright light of the moon. The smell of hot dogs and pizza lingered in the air; here and there mice grabbed morsels of food that had been dropped on the ground.

"It looks creepy, doesn't it? So different when there aren't any bright lights or music playing or people walking around," Lisa said.

Jeff looked around. "Yeah, it's weird. But still kinda cool." He took Lisa's face in his hands. "You're so beautiful in the moonlight," he whispered. Then he laughed. "Romantic, huh?"

She rolled her eyes. "No, ridiculous. Who are you supposed to be, Romeo?"

"Who?"

"Geez, no wonder you're failing your literature class. Come on; kiss me since we have to get out of here soon. I'd rather not miss my curfew again."

They were really into it when Lisa felt a tickling on her leg. She broke away from Jeff and saw a spider climbing up her thigh. With a squeal, she smacked it off, launching it into the air. "Let's go, Jeff! It's getting colder and there are bugs around. Why would a spider be way up here anyway?"

"Yeah, all right." He grabbed the metal bar to pull himself out of the car when there was a loud metal clang. They looked down to see a man hit the ride with a baseball bat, repeating the loud noise.

"Hey, you kids! What the hell are you doing on my Ferris wheel? Git yer asses down here right now!'

Before they could move, he threw a switch and the ride jerked and rocked, bringing the kids down slowly. By the time their car reached the bottom, Lisa was crying.

"This ain't no place for a couple of stupid kids right now. Don't you know all kinds of things can happen after dark in a place like this? Now go home before you regret you didn't."

Lisa sniffled and wiped her nose on her jacket. "Sorry, mister."

"Yeah, sorry," Jeff mumbled. "Come on, Lisa. We don't want to piss off any *spooks* that might be around." He waved his arms in the air and made a scary face. Lisa smiled through her tears. Jeff was so cool.

"Don't say I didn't warn you. Just git yourselves home and everything will be fine." The man glared at them and then walked back to the tent, shaking his head and muttering under his breath.

Jeff watched him go. "Stupid old man. Trying to scare us." Jeff had been startled when the man banged on the ride, but didn't show it. Now he was more irritated than scared. "Let's go look around a little bit. That jerk can't tell us what to do."

"Are you crazy?" Lisa looked at Jeff in disbelief. "I'm going home before that guy calls the cops or something."

"He's not gonna call the cops, especially if the workers have been stealing from people. He's just trying to scare us into leaving. This place seems really cool at night—remember how it looked from the Ferris wheel? I want to explore a little. We'll just stay away from that tent."

Lisa desperately wanted to leave, but she didn't want Jeff to think she was a baby. She'd been wanting to go out with him for a long time, and she was finally with him. Her mom thought he was a bad influence, and maybe her mom was right, but nothing was going to stop her from hanging out with him.

"Okay," she said. "But only for a little while. If I get home after curfew again, I'll be worse than grounded."

Jeff pulled on Lisa's arm. "Come on, I'll get you a stuffed animal."

"But that's stealing, Jeff! Let's just go look at the other rides or something." Lisa knew Jeff had gotten caught shoplifting once, and didn't want him to get arrested for taking something as lame as a stuffed animal.

"Shh! Just come on."

They walked quietly through the grounds. The carnival had a different feel when there were no people around; it was eerie, too silent. The animals on the carousel seemed alive, as if ready to break free. Even the kiddie rides were different; the cheerful little bug cars that were charming when the carnival was lit up became menacing under the moonlight.

"I really don't like this place, Jeff. I feel like we're being watched or something. What if that guy is following us?"

"I know, it feels kind of creepy to me too. Let's get out of here. But I don't want to go back the way we came just in case that guy's following us. He might actually call the cops if he sees we're still here. I don't need that hassle again. We'll head out past the Tilt-a-Whirl."

They walked for a few minutes, passing by the bumper cars and the funhouse, as well as the cotton candy stand. Jeff stopped and looked around uncertainly.

"I could've sworn the Tilt-a-Whirl was around here. I rode it a few days ago with my little brother. I remember it was right next to the funhouse."

"It's somewhere else then, but I don't remember where. The carnival isn't *that* big; it's got to be nearby. We just took a wrong turn or something."

They headed back and turned past the haunted house. The fronts of the game booths were covered with tarps but loosely draped.

"Oh, wait a minute," he said, his uncertainty momentarily forgotten. "I wanted to grab a stuffed animal for you. There's the dart game booth; they always have good prizes for that one."

"Oh, God. Can we just go, please?" Lisa had finally had enough and didn't care if Jeff got mad at her. "I don't care about a stupid stuffed animal."

Jeff ignored her, and moved the tarp aside. He spied a bunch of stuffed animals hanging on a wall in the dark booth and stretched his arm to grab a teddy bear. Suddenly he snatched his hand back.

"Damn, I think I scratched my hand on a nail or something." He looked at his palm. There was a long scratch on it, with little beads of blood popping to the surface. It stung, making him forget about the teddy bear. He looked through the tarp, but didn't see any nails poking out. He was trying figure out what had scratched him when Lisa grabbed his arm, hurting him.

"Jeff!'

"Ow! Damn it! What is *wrong* with you?"

"I saw someone peeking around the fried-Oreo stand over there. It might've been that creepy jerk. I knew he was following us!'

"Oh, what the hell?" This night wasn't turning out at all the way Jeff had hoped. "Hey!" he yelled. "We said we're leaving; just give us the chance to get out!'

Jeff then saw the face Lisa had seen. It wasn't the old man, it was one of the clowns that roamed the carnival, bugging people and giving away balloons. Little kids thought the clowns were great; Jeff hated them. They creeped him out. The clown stepped out from behind the cookie booth, giving Jeff a better look at him. Why was the clown out this time of night, and why was he still in costume? And his costume was all dirty—the white suit had dark stains all over it that almost looked like blood. In fact, Jeff thought he could actually smell blood—a rank, coppery smell that caught in his throat and almost made him gag.

The clown caught Jeff's eye and waved at him with a shriveled hand. The fingernails looked like claws, thin, long and black. Then the clown grinned—and all Jeff could see were *teeth*. Big teeth, yellow and sharp, that looked like needles.

"Oh, God ... we really need to go right *now*, Lisa. There's something wrong with that clown."

Lisa looked again toward the fried-Oreo booth. Her eyes widened with horror. "Run!'

They took off running, racing back toward the Ferris wheel, hoping to get out the way they came in.

"Where's the damn Ferris wheel?" Lisa was crying again, and she didn't care about Jeff thinking she was a baby. She was terrified.

They saw it looming ominously in the distance above the other rides but couldn't find where it was grounded. They couldn't get any closer to it no matter how far they ran.

"This is crazy!" Jeff was scared and frustrated and just wanted to go home. He regretted not stealing the farmer's tractor in the first place. He didn't feel like such a badass right now.

As Jeff was silently cursing himself, the clown jumped out from behind the candy apple stand right in front of them. Jeff stumbled against Lisa, making her fall on the rough dirt surface. She lifted her head in time to see the clown roll a bright red ball toward them. It landed in front of her and exploded into hundreds of tiny spiders.

Lisa tried to get up, but before she could, spiders scuttled up her arms and into her hair. She stood up, frantically raking her fingers through her hair.

"Get them off, get them off!" she screamed.

"Get what off?"

"Spiders! They're all over me!'

Jeff looked at her, but he didn't see any spiders. And now the clown was gone, as if he hadn't even been there. "There's nothing on you! Shit, where'd the clown go?"

"I don't know and I don't care—I just want to go home! This place is scary and there's something wrong here. I *know* those spiders were climbing on me."

Jeff gently smoothed Lisa's hair. "We'll find our way out, don't worry. I know it's weird around here, but I bet the carnival workers are just trying to scare us for trespassing."

"But the spiders—"

"You imagined them. Maybe the clown played a trick on you. But whatever, they aren't there now. Come on, let's go."

Lisa closed her eyes and inhaled deeply. "I *didn't* imagine them, but fine, I'm ready."

She grabbed Jeff's hand and tried to walk on, but he didn't move. She looked over to prod him on but saw it wasn't Jeff's hand she had taken.

It was the clown's.

She screamed and dropped the clown's hand, his nails scraping her wrist, drawing blood. She ran through the carnival, his laughter following her.

Lisa ducked into the first tent she came to. She hadn't seen it when she and Jeff were walking around trying to find their way out. It smelled odd, somewhat musty. The tent was empty except for cobwebs covering the walls. She put her hands on her knees and bent over, trying to catch her breath. She wanted to leave the tent and try to find her way home, but she was scared the clown was waiting outside for her. She didn't feel safe in the tent, either; the cobwebs frightened her and gave her the creeps the way they were fluttering without any wind. Suddenly she heard the clown's laughter; this time it was all around her. She looked around but didn't see him.

"Please leave me alone!" she sobbed. "I'm sorry we messed around with your carnival! I'll never do it again. Please just let me go home!'

She felt a tap on her shoulder and knew the clown was behind her. She closed her eyes and clenched her fists, hoping he'd disappear. She whispered a prayer, knowing it wouldn't be heard. She felt herself being turned around; she was helpless to stop. The clown now stood in front of her, baring his teeth. Then he opened his mouth wide and roared, exhaling hundreds of spiders. They hit Lisa's face, climbing into her mouth when she opened it to scream. They slid down her throat, choking her. She fell to her knees, clawing at her neck, trying to cough them out.

Darkness overtook her and she mercifully knew no more.

Jeff couldn't understand how he'd gotten separated from Lisa. He'd seen that damned clown again, and it had caught him off-guard. He'd nearly fallen and realized Lisa had. But when he went to pull her up, his hand had taken that of the clown's instead, and he ran as fast as he could to get away, all thoughts of Lisa gone.

Now he felt like a coward, leaving her behind. *You're such an asshole,* he thought. He walked back to find Lisa but heard the clown's laughter all around him. He froze in place and looked around. Jeff took a few cautious steps forward and then heard a noise behind him.

He whipped around, but nothing was there. He turned back to search for Lisa and found himself face to face with the clown.

The clown put his face right up to Jeff's, held Jeff's chin in his hand and ran his slimy tongue along the side of Jeff's face. Jeff wet his pants, but he didn't care. He tried to turn and run, but the clown grabbed him by the throat and lifted him off the ground, holding him in the air. The clown tilted his head left, then right, as he stared into Jeff's eyes. He threw Jeff to the ground and dragged him by his shirt through the carnival, Jeff pulling at the clown's hands on his collar all the while. Then the clown pulled him inside a run-down tent and threw Jeff to the ground.

Jeff saw Lisa lying motionless on the ground, her face frozen in a silent scream, with only the whites of her eyes showing. A spider crawled out of her mouth while Jeff looked on, horrified.

"You're next," the clown whispered in his ear, running a fingernail down the side of Jeff's face.

Lisa's body suddenly began to shake, then violently erupted

with hundreds of spiders. They swarmed as they ate their way through her flesh, trailing blood and tissue. They skittered toward Jeff, who lay helpless as they bit him and tore at his flesh, while the clown laughed and clapped his hands.

The carnies played poker and threw back whiskey shots in their tent, laughing at each other's raunchy jokes.

The Ferris wheel carnie shushed them. "Did you hear that? I thought I heard a scream." He stood up and listened. Yes, there it was again. Definitely a scream; someone was in trouble or hurt. He worried it was one of the kids he had chased off earlier. He'd given them a chance to get away from the carnival, but maybe they didn't take it.

"We told you before to let it go, Stan."

"But that's the third time this month it's happened. What can we do?" Stanley had only joined up with the carnival a few months before and still didn't understand the way of things.

"Trust me—we don't get involved. Bad things happen. Just drink your whiskey. It'll be quiet again soon."

Stan reluctantly sat back down, trying not to hear the terrified screams echoing in the night, and pretending he hadn't seen a sharp-toothed clown peeking at him from around the tents.

And finally, I reviewed an anthology published in 2010 called Machine of Death, edited by Ryan North. The common theme throughout was that a machine was built with a needle inside that would prick your finger, test the blood, and give you a piece of paper that would tell you how you would die. Not when, though. And the word(s) on the paper could mean anything. "Comet" didn't necessarily mean the Earth would be struck—you could slip on some Comet cleanser while you were mopping the floor and crack your head. It was an amazing collection of stories, So when they put out a call for submissions for the second book, I wrote a story for it. Unfortunately, it wasn't accepted. I was disappointed, but I knew my chances were slim—they received over 2,000 submissions. Although the title is a little titillating, it's not a graphic sex story.

ORGASM

Christina was still chuckling a little as she pulled in the driveway of her two-story home. Stopping by the Machine of Death had been daring, cathartic. Jake had forbidden her to take the test, and in a rare show of secret rebellion, she pricked her finger while running errands. The Machine was located in almost every grocery store these days; Christina made sure she went to the other side of town where nobody knew her.

She must have passed the Machine ten times before working up the nerve to do it. Each time she approached it, goose bumps appeared on her arms and her mouth went dry. She wasn't sure what she was more scared of—the answer or her husband's reaction if he were to find out what she had done. Finally, she stuck her finger in. A quick pinch, a whirring sound, and then the card was spit out into the tray.

ORGASM, it read.

Are you KIDDING me? Christina stood in front of the Machine, gawking at her destiny.

"Hey, lady—get out of the way. My kid here wants to give it a go."

Snapping out of her shock, Christina grabbed her cart and resumed shopping, leaving the cranky lady and her little boy behind. Suddenly, she was struck with a case of the giggles in the produce section.

Orgasm? Christina hadn't had one in years. She had long since closed herself off from her emotions when it came to sex with Jake. Oh, she faked it; if Jake thought he hadn't satisfied her, he'd feel all insecure and take it out on her. So she went through the motions, even though her skin crawled and her stomach roiled. Christina was so sexually dead inside she didn't even bother to satisfy herself. No, ORGASM was not something she needed to fear anytime soon.

She tossed the card in the trashcan on her way out.

"You're late." Jake sat at the kitchen table, beer in hand and smoking a joint. "You know you're supposed to come home right from the store."

"Oh, there were only a couple checkers at the market and lots of people. I'm really sorry, Jake." Christina's voice trembled slightly. "Let me fix you some dinner."

"Damn right you will. Hurry up; I'm going out tonight."

"Um, okay—where are you going, honey?" Christina's hands shook as she rummaged through the bags, putting groceries away.

"None of your business. I'll be home late."

Christina lay on her side of the bed, crying. She knew Jake was with another woman. He frequently was. She could always smell it on him. She didn't care so much that he was having sex with someone else; usually he left her alone when he came home on those nights. But why wouldn't he let her go? Why did he insist on making her stay if he wanted other women?

The bedroom door suddenly flew open and slammed against the wall. Jake stumbled in, stinking of booze and perfume. "Hey, baby," he purred, taking off his shirt. "How's about a little sweetness for your lover?"

Oh, God, please no. Not tonight.

But Christina had no choice. As Jake moved on top of her, mumbling drunkenly and kissing her face sloppily, Christina squeezed her eyes shut and tried to pretend it wasn't happening. Finally Jake rolled off her, passed out and snoring.

Christina took a hot shower and then cried herself to sleep, but she woke up with a plan.

The next morning, Christina made bacon and eggs for Jake, his favorite. He demanded a hot-cooked breakfast every morning before work. She heard him slowly make his way down the stairs; she poured hot coffee and handed him the cup as he walked into the kitchen.

"How are you this morning? You were pretty hammered when you came in." Christina wasn't worried about angering Jake right now; his hangovers made him pretty mellow for a while. She almost liked him the morning after a big drunk.

"God, my head is pounding. Give me some aspirin, will ya?" Jake squeezed his wife's neck affectionately, although a little hard. Christina winced and got the aspirin.

"Jake, how about if you and I stay in tonight and have dinner together? We haven't done that in so long, and I'd love for us to talk—maybe snuggle together in bed. I'll make your favorite and we'll share a bottle of wine. What do you say? Please?" Christina smiled up at Jake, but the smile didn't make it to her eyes.

"Sure, baby. I guess I can give you a night. Not much going on down at Cooper's tonight anyway." He sat down and ate his breakfast, pointing his knife at her as he talked. "Wear that nightie I got you—I want to see you cooking in it. And put on some heels with it—you're gonna strut for me." He leered at her, his mouth full of eggs. Christina suppressed a shudder.

"All right, I'm gone, girl." Jake picked up his lunch cooler and headed out the door.

Christina went back to the grocery store to pick up the steak and potatoes for dinner. And just to be sure, she put her finger in the Machine of Death again.

ORGASM.

Satisfied, Christina also picked up a bottle of wine and her Valium prescription. Jake had no clue she took Valium; he would be furious. She tried not to take it all the time, but sometimes she just needed it.

She would need it tonight.

They sat at the dining room table, something they hadn't done for a long time. Although Jake was in a grumpy mood, Christina was determined tonight would work out.

"What do you say we take the rest of the wine upstairs?" Christina smiled, looking beautiful in her lingerie and heels. She had pinned her hair up; she knew Jake liked to take it down when he kissed her.

Jake grumbled, "Whatever, I guess." Then he leered at her. "I'm going to rip that nightie right off you, girl." He grabbed a bottle of Jack off the counter and headed upstairs.

"I'll be up in a minute," Christina called after him. She quickly finished her glass of wine and poured more. Then she got the sandwich bag of Valium she had crushed up earlier and shook it into the wine glass, stirring it with her finger. She knew it was enough for a lethal overdose.

She downed it, grimacing at the bitter taste. She left the glass, now coated with Valium residue, on the table and headed upstairs.

Jake was waiting in bed, naked and drinking from the bottle of Jack. "Come here, baby," he said, slurring his words. "Take a drink."

Christina's stomach was already upset from the combination of food, drugs, and alcohol. She didn't want to drink the Jack and then throw up the Valium. She knew she wasn't going to die from it, but she needed to keep it in her body.

"No, let's just make love, sweetie," she said. She took off her nightie and walked across the room to him.

"I said *take a drink.*" Jake's voice was menacing; Christina knew she had to placate him or her plan wouldn't work. She took a quick sip of the whiskey and shuddered. Jake laughed and pulled her to him. "That's what I'm talkin' about, baby." He kissed her, and for the first time in a long time, she kissed him back. Surprised, Jake held her close, almost tenderly.

Tonight those walls she had kept up for years were coming down. She was going to enjoy sex for the last time.

ORGASM, the card had read. The card she had torn up and thrown away while at the store that morning.

The Valium wasn't going to kill her. But Jake wouldn't know that. And neither would the police.

About the Author

Sheri White has lived in Maryland all her life and has the crab-picking skills and the big can of Old Bay in her pantry to show for it.

Her stories have been published in many anthologies, including Be Very Afraid (edited by Edo Van Belkom), Decadence 2 (edited by Monica J. O'Rourke), Once Upon an Apocalypse (edited by Scott Goudsward and Rachel Kenley), and Fresh Blood, Old Bones (edited by Kasey Lansdale). Magazine appearances include Lamplight, The Sirens Call, Devolution Z, and Beware the Dark.

She is also the editor of the UK magazine Morpheus Tales.

Find her on Facebook:

https://www.facebook.com/sheriw1965

Curious about other Crossroad Press books?
Stop by our site:
http://store.crossroadpress.com
We offer quality writing
in digital, audio, and print formats.

Enter the code FIRSTBOOK
to get 20% off your first order from our store!
Stop by today!